MORT AND BLACKIE

A Comic Mystery

Michael N. Felix

Mort and Blackie

Books by Michael N. Felix

The Marsh Birds

New Babylon Road

Milo Mudd

The Weather Witch

Mort and Blackie

Heart of the North (Short Stories)

Ma Ka To (Pending Publication)

Poems from the Road

A Note from the Author

I have long been a fan of the great crime and mystery writers of America, beginning with Edgar Allen Poe. I read Dashiel Hammett and, my favorite, Ray Chandler, along with the modern greats; Elmore Leonard and James Elroy, and others..

One winter, totally for fun, between episodes of mild insanity known as mountain climbing, I wrote the first draft of Mort and Blackie. It was conceived of as a story of two rooky detectives solving crime.. But really my intention was to poke fun at various institutions, the press, books, traffic, old hippy guys…, really anything else that happened to be in the newspaper on the day I was writing.

Lots of people seem to like Mortimer Jablonsky and John Blackman. At any rate here is the first book. There is a second book, most of which is still in my head. In that spirit, here it is. Luck to you.

Michael N. Felix, Florida Mtns, NM, February, 2019

One

Chief Powell was a little straight-backed man, and when he really got mad he strutted nervously up and down the expensive carpet in front of the huge window overlooking his domain talking in spitters and sputters and little eruptions as if he were a miniature volcano unable to explode all in one blast.

His present eruptive fury was directed at two sheepish looking young men seated in front of the vast expanse of his desk. The first of the young men, Mortimer E. Jablonsky, who was very large, calm and somewhat soft looking, ran a hand through his fine long brown hair and tried to look meek. This effort at lessening his profile only made him seem somewhat like a pinstriped and sheepish whale."But Uncle Powell…," implored Mortie. "We were just trying to help. We ….."

Chief Powell whirled around and shot a look at him. "And don't uncle me, Jablonsky. I've told you about that. We'll have some professionalism here if nothing else."

Next to Mortie sat John Blackman, tiny and twitchy, seemingly incapable of sitting still for more than a few seconds. For quite a while he had been, through strenuous mental effort, attempting to look innocent by edging toward

Mortie's shadow and trying to memorize the tips of his highly polished shoes.

It didn't work.

"And that goes for you too, Blackman," said Chief Powell, stepping around the desk and pointing a stubby finger at him. "Goes double if you ask me,"

Mortie shifted uneasily. "Well… See…, Blackie here…. He…. It really wasn't his….., his….."

"Quiet you….!" yelled Chief Powell. The chief held his hands in front of himself and shook them as if he were trying to get water off of his fingers and then suddenly stuck his jaw out at the two erstwhile detectives. "A frontend loader!" he said. "What in the heck were you thinking for God's sake? I let you two clowns hang around a bust to get a little experience and you drive a frontend loader through a wall?"

Mortie had seen this sort of thing before and was counting on the fact that the volcano would most likely die down in a while. At least he hoped this was the case. You could never tell what Chief Powell would do. I know it for a fact that he had once thrown a chair down a staircase in a rage; which wouldn't have been so bad, except that the chair had been occupied when he threw it. That had been in the days of the Chief's impulsive youth, so to speak, as a police commander. Recently he had mellowed somewhat. Still one couldn't be certain, so Mortie just sat there squirming and trying to appeal to his uncle with his soulful brown eyes. This tactic had worked before and it might work again.

Besides there didn't seem to be any alternative readily at hand.

The Chief offered a beseeching prayer at the ceiling. "The Mayor called!" he exclaimed. "God I'm dead."

Mortie folded his perfectly clean but chubby hands on his lap as if he were in church and then snuck a look over at Blackie. No help there. He turned his eyes back to his uncle.

"Well.... See, Uncle Fred ..."

At this the chief abruptly stopped him with a raised palm.

"Don't you listen....? Do not, under any circumstances 'uncle' me."

"Sorry, Chief Sir," started Mortie again. "It wasn't the wall we busted down. See we saw the Swat team wasn't getting into the building and Blackie here, he..." Mort looked over in the general direction of Blackie who had at that moment, shifted his attention to the rather ornate toe of the leg of the Chief's giant mahogany desk in an attempt to be still.

Impossible.

All of Blackie's lean and middle-sized body (He had once boxed though he was better at eluding than punching.) fidgeted and moved constantly, rather like an actor in one of those old time movies. The most you could say for him was that he was active.

He shifted around nervously and then cleared his throat.

"See, Chief," he began. "I think what Mortie here was trying to say was that - what we were doing was -" He looked a little wildly at Mort, and his small hands lifted off as if of their own volition and began darting around in the air. Blackie's hands were tiny compared to Mort's and almost preternaturally dexterous, and one would have thought him delicate if he didn't virtually always wear black t-shirts showing rather substantial biceps. The t-shirts would seem to indicate an aggressive sort of person which he wasn't. Seeing that he had the floor, so to speak, Blackie began to warm up to his memory of the events of the previous night.

"What we had here, Chief, was an emergency," he began reasonably. Mortie nodded vigorously in agreement. "Whatchyoucall your real emergency," he went on. "And then I saw this frontend loader. It didn't have a key in it, so I hotwired it and drove it across the street to the building..... Then I used one fork to sort of forklift the door open......"

The Chief snorted and abruptly held out his hand in a stop gesture.

"I'm not sure I want to hear this. I might have to book the both of you. Emergency...? Emergency my rear end... Which, I might add by the way, is in a sling. I'm the one with the emergency! The Mayor called! And now he's going to call back. Do you two idiots hear me?!" he exclaimed. "The Mayor!" He clutched his head, trying apparently to calm himself by the simple expedient of grasping his head with both hands. He sighed.

"And me with a year and a half to retirement," he said in exasperation. "My god...." Suddenly, thinking of something else, he abruptly turned his blockish jaw toward Blackie. "How in heck do you hotwire a frontend loader that quickly anyway, huh? Tell me that! What are you anyway? In some criminal gang yourself in your time off?"

Blackie, to whom the idea of a rhetorical question did not exist, still managed to keep from saying anything. For his part Chief Powell continued to stalk back and forth muttering something about not going down with the ship.

The Chief stopped his pacing. Seeing this, Blackie thought he was off the hook. But Chief Powell stopped, spun on a heel, turned and glared at him.

"Well?"

Blackie looked back blankly. "What?"

"Well Mr. Genius, how do you do it?"

Blackie thought it best to approach this question carefully. "Well sir.... It's really not that hard.... I was probably just lucky. They're—uh --- simple." His hands flew up again like illustrating butterflies. "You just rip out the positive, that's usually the black wire.... and then.... If you're in a hurry that is..." He looked at the chief eagerly.

"He can hot-wire anything in thirty seconds or less, boss," chimed in Mortie. "He's the best."

At this Blackie shook his head in modesty, waving a hand. "It's nothing really.... I..."

But the Chief wanted no more.

"Shut up, Blackman," he said. "And you too Mortie. I don't want to know. Hot-wiring a frontend loader....!" He rolled his eyes and lifted one beseeching palm to the ceiling, then flopped uncomfortably in the leather chair behind his desk. He stared balefully across the desk...

"If I hadn't promised my brother I'd take care of you, Mortie… I'd. ….. I'd …" he started. "How you two ever managed to make it through the police academy I'll never know. The two of you couldn't rake leaves and get it done right."

At the words *rake* and *leaves* the Chief went suddenly silent. A curtain seemed to fall in front of his gaze, behind which glowed a light, the light of an idea...; a very good idea. He settled into a sommnabulatory silence. He twiddled with one of his pens. Mortie watched this sudden alteration in his uncle, not to mention the pen twiddling, with a horrible sense of foreboding. He thought that perhaps they should leave. Maybe if they were out of sight….. He started to get up, gesturing all the while toward the door.

"Well, Chief Sir," he said. "It looks as if you want to be alone so we'll just…."

But Chief Powell stopped him with an abrupt downward gesture.

"Sit….!," he ordered. He resumed his contemplation. You see, the Chief, though no genius, had not climbed the long bureaucratic ladder of the city up to Chiefhood by making ill-advised moves. Step by step he had advanced. And very early he had realized a fact, a certainty that is true about all organizations, the higher one climbs, the narrower and more crowded the path. He had once been a rough-and-ready patrolman, but annoyingly, somewhere along the line, had realized that, as you rose higher you actually had to think about each thing you do. Seemingly innocuous decisions often caused unexpected results. Still it had all worked out. He was virtually assured of a comfortable retirement.

But he wanted more. He desperately wanted that thing his predecessor had gotten.

The Silver Mug…Solid silver! Well, not really, but it was the idea, you understand, not the fact that was important. It meant… He had tried not to dwell on it, but it was always in his head and he wanted that one important thing it meant.

Respect.

He had been thinking about that silver mug a lot these days. He had made few bad decisions but one of them, or at least one he hadn't expected, was sitting in front of him, in the form of his nephew. Mortie had been one of those unexpected phenomenon. There was an ugly word for it. Nepotism. He had, he cringed at the thought, actually encouraged his brother to let Mortie take the civil service test and apply to the academy.

Who would have expected that Mortie would not fail? If not the written test, then the physical and discipline regime of the academy. That was certain. But to his shock Mortie had passed it all. Not only had he passed the test, but he had passed it with a high score…. One of the highest scores! And not only that, but as a patrolman he had, if not an exemplary record, but…for he was a leisurely sort of officer, more prone to chatting with locals at the coffee shop than wildly chasing down perpetrators. Though he was a big man, he was very soft looking and benign in temperament. His sole unusual physical talent was an incredible strength in his hands and arms. This was a natural strength. He had never lifted weights or squeezed springs or anything else and he did not demonstrate this strength, though once he bent back the top part of a damaged car door to help a man exit the vehicle, while the other officer gaped. Amazingly, he had calmed a particularly violent ward of the city. The people had actually asked for Mortie to return.

"Unusual and unorthodox but gets the job done," said Farley Snodgrass, Section Chief, who he, the Chief, suspected of simply passing Mortie through to annoy him. He grimaced at the thought of Snodgrass….. That red hair. Always going around grinning and braying like an ass. Probably wanted his job.

Mortie and Blackie had partnered up after their orientation. Blackie drove his older partners crazy with his gadgets. Mortie used technology, but it wasn't an abiding interest. They were thus natural partners. Chief Powell had no idea where Blackie had appeared from though he suspected some other planet.

"Uh Chief….," a nasally Brooklyn accent interrupted his reverie.

"Yes, Alice?" said Chief Powell.

Alice Birdwright, his secretary, her hair like a reddish explosion of static electricity, had stuck her head in the door. Electric Alice…., loved gossip, knew how to keep her mouth shut, queen of her domain and knew it, with a shark's smile as bright as tooth whitener could getem. Smart as a whip and twice as brash, the Chief's daily schedule memorized, a pen stuck behind an ear…; among her other duties she was Chief Powell's Executive Assistant, Political Advisor, extractor when he needed to be yanked, smoother-outer of awkward imbroglios and his Sharp Knife when something needed cutting…, or someone needed to be cut loose... In short, she was his Fixer when something needed fixing. And when she fixed em, they usually stayed fixed.

"It's the Maya for yis again, Cheef," she announced.

The Chief stared at the black phone on his desk as if it were some wild animal about to pounce. On the fifth ring he snatched it up.

"Mayor!" he fairly yelled. "How are you? How's the wife? Can I…? I can assure …… Yes, yes, we're still looking into the matter. Well of course I'm on top of it. And I can assure you that it will never happen aga……."

He held the phone away from his ear.

"Yes.., yes…, yes, yes, yes sir,….. yes, yes, mayor sir… They won't be.. You can be assured of……." But apparently the Mayor had hung up. The Chief stared at the phone.

This was bad.

Mortie racked his brain desperately, but his brain, normally a calm and clear thinking logical organ, suddenly turned fickle and chose this moment to abandon him. Across the room a fly buzzed, decided somewhere in its fly brain that the window it was trying to get out through wasn't going to work, and that another window might just be the ticket. Lifting off from where it was idling its engines, it buzzed erratically across the giant ocean of the room toward another light, or warmth or whatever a fly is looking for; perhaps another fly. One doesn't know. Unfortunately for the fly, the erratic trajectory of its trans-office path passed too close to Blackie.

Snap!

With an idle, but incredibly fast movement he snatched the fly out of the air. This was for Blackie the sort of automatic sort of thing he did without thinking. The fly now buzzed indignantly in his fist. Blackie considered the poor beast through a peephole between thumb and forefinger. Feeling a gaze he glanced up.

He froze.

Blackie's lightning movement had broken the Chief's reverie and he was now staring at Blackie with acute displeasure. As if sensing an ally, albeit one so inept as not to be able to do the simple trick of landing on a ceiling, the fly buzzed angrily and energetically in his fist. Reluctant to murder the poor insect, for he was the sort of person who had a great sympathy for all things small and quick in spirit, Blackie just sat there. The Chief nodded his head imperceptibly toward the door. Gingerly, with the Chief's eyes boring into his back, Blackie walked to the door and tossed the fly into the air of the outer office. Shocked at its sudden freedom, the fly did nothing for a split second, and then revved up its little engine, regained its bearings and headed off toward the coffee bar for a light repast.

Somewhere in the outer office a phone was ringing and ringing. Mortie had located a fingernail file and was touching up his immaculate nails. Chief Powell, having observed all of this with an air of infinite but unsurprised disgust, leaned forward onto the desk and made a little tent of his fingers.

"Well, well, well.....," he started. "If Mr. Nature lover and you, the movie star don't mind sparing the time I have an idea." He motioned toward Blackie who was creeping back toward his seat. "Siddown, Blackman." He smiled. "It's this. See the problem here as I see it is this....We've got to get you out of sight for a few weeks...Don't you agree boys..?"

This horribly pleasant look on his uncle's face was so alarming a sight to Mortie that he knew he had to do *something.* He didn't know where this turnpike was going but he didn't think he wanted to take the trip. He shifted uncomfortably.

"Uhhh... uncle," he started. "I don't think....."

But the Chief held up his hand to stop him. "Can it, Mortie.... I like this one.... I have a place you boys can go for a nice long stretch of getting out of my hair. The Parks Department... A fine idea, don't you think?"

Mort and Blackie stared.

The Chief got up and strode happily to a window gesturing in the general direction of Riverside Park. "You boys know my friend Katzman? …. Eh boys….?"

Two

Riverside Park, a fine and large expanse of rolling grass and woods, stretched languidly along the muddy river for several miles… Fat here, and narrow there, it was shaped somewhat like a python that had consumed two or three unfortunate animals. It was a place of rolling hills, trees galore, flowers and ponds, with a nice sprinkling of muggers to keep things interesting. There was even an idyllic little pond with two strips of new grass leading to it, where the tracks of the street sweeper had been erased through intense effort – the type of effort only generated by a temporarily desperate politician with minions galore under him. Thoreau would have been proud.

Mortie and Blackie were sitting in some shade, Mortie on an ancient serape' an aunt had given him. Long ago, she had visited the border states of Mexico and had mistaken the smoky, enterprising gleam in the eyes of the locals as… friendship. As a result of these expeditions, she had returned with enough bric-a-brac and indigenous clothing to stock a warehouse.

It had been nine days. Nine brain-boiling hot days. This was the hottest. Mortie glanced up at the giant yellow sun glaring down at them, unmoving in the clear, blue sky.

"This is it…" he said.

"What?" said Blackie, who was seated half in the shade, and was squinting at a tiny computer balanced on his feet in front of him. He was typing away at something.

"The lowest point in my life," said Mortie, tugging at his sweaty work uniform.

Blackie squinted more at his tiny computer. He lifted it and turned it side to side, and then hunched down under a towel, to get a better look at something on the screen. "Did you know that this park is famous for its flowers?"

"Yes, of course," Mortie said irritably. "There's a spring flower festival. It's known all over."

Blackie looked up happily. "I like flowers. And they do sculling on the river! But that's later in July."

Mortie shuddered at the thought of himself in a skinny little boat. He glanced at his watch, sighed, and bleakly surveyed the vast green expanse of the park. Time to go back to work. Except for the breaks and the half hour off for lunch periods when time zipped merrily along, time had somehow ceased its ceaseless, forward march.

His life had stopped. In a while, they slowly got up and went back to work. Technically, they were there as undercover police. They had thought that perhaps the undisputed fact of their being policemen would somehow allow them to take a more casual view of this assignment. Blackie was energetic at any hour, but Mortie's idea of something to do at seven in the morning was to have coffee and read a newspaper in his bathrobe. Mortie had even conjured up a vision; a leisurely breakfast wherein he could read the morning Herald. Perhaps, were he in a hurry, a coffee to go at his favorite on-the-move coffee place, Hassan's Hot Coffee. Hassan's was up on Wheelock, an unpretentious kiosk on an unpaved parking lot next to a very busy boulevard. Hassan himself would whoosh out the special of the day, his favorite, a double Turkish Espresso in hot sugary cream, with a dusting of cinnamon. All you needed to keep you yammering for hours. Mortie never yammered, but you get the point.

It wasn't to be.

There had been strict orders from on high that they would work exactly like every other parks worker, emphasis on the word "worker." Any observing they would do would be done from that cover. And from this work they had learned two brutal things about parks workers. The first is that every bucolic scene gets to be bucolic by the sweat of some minion's brow. The other brutal reality of their job was the shocking hour they began this labor. Shortly after the birds leaped from their nests chirping morosely to greet the new day, the parks workers limped out to start their day.

It had started the first morning. Ortiz, the foreman, a very polite, soft spoken, squatty little man with very opaque black eyes, held out some sort of hideous clothing.

"Wear these," he said to Mortie, handing him a jumpsuit of the sort that mechanics, or in this case, convicts, no longer used.

"Do we have to…?" said Mortie, handling his coverall as if it had come in recent contact with the plague.

Ortiz smiled emptily. He nodded. "Mr. Katzman likes 'em. He can see everyone easier. Without the eye strain."

Mortie tugged fruitlessly at his uniform. The jumpsuit covered him completely and once had been orange… or some color similar to orange… at any rate, a very bright orange, a luminescent orange designed to be visible in almost any level of light. Somehow the orange color, despite innumerable washings, or the desperate perspirations of the previous occupants, had not faded. *Dept. of Corr.* was stenciled in faded letters across the back shoulders of each suit.

Rivers of sweat poured off his dripping brow. His uniform was too small at the shoulders and the crotch pinched in, forcing him to walk slightly bent so that he looked like a luminescent orange Sasquatch.

Blackie came jogging up. His uniform was exactly the same size as Mortie's, so that he had had to roll up both the pant legs and the sleeves. He didn't seem to mind.

"Isn't this great?!" he exclaimed, looking around and encompassing the sky in a grand gesture. "What a day!"

Mortie, whose idea of fresh air was visiting an old bookstore, frowned at him. "No…" he said. "It ain't… isn't," he corrected himself. He looked around pathetically.

"All right!" yelled Ortiz. "We got four hundred geraniums in just last night that got to be put in the ground. We're getting ready for ta Festival of Flowers. It's big this year and the mayor is hot about it. So there's more coming in. It's gettin' warm now, so the quicker the better, and make sure you water all of them in." Later, Mortie, who liked flowers, decided he hated Azaleas. "Where in heck do they get all of these flowers?" he asked.

"Texas or somewhere like that, I hear," said a skinny kid, his baseball cap jammed backward onto his head. "They grow them there. The season's longer there, so they're shipped up from there – or maybe China…."

Blackie jogged off toward where some other workers were gathered.

Mortie leaned his rake against a huge old oak. He was extremely hot. His face felt flushed. Heat stroke, he felt, was a possibility. He had heard about this. He itched all over. He held the rake in two hands and tried to use it as a giant back scratcher. Still, he itched. He shook himself and twisted around, trying to reach a spot in the middle of his back that had been itching for the last ten minutes. This not working, he looked around carefully to see if anyone was watching, then peeled back the top half of the bright orange jump-suit, backed up to a tree, and began rubbing up and down against the oak, much in the manner of a bear scratching itself. A look of utter bliss shown on his face. In a while, he and the tree had had enough.

He glanced at his watch. Nine o'clock. Still! He looked up and shaded his eyes, examining the sky hopefully. Perhaps rain… None. He examined the terrain toward the river in hopes that some suspicious miscreant might give him an excuse to become a policeman again. Off in the extreme verges of the china blue sky, one powder puff cloud sailed serenely along. He thought with regret of all the cooling rainstorms he had taken for granted or worse, as a hindrance. He had never realized before how much he loved lightning. He shoehorned himself back into his sweaty suit and picked up his rake. Surveying the ten feet of verdure in front of him, he selected some grass cuttings and, using some tines of the rake, he began to gather these cuttings together. Working slowly and very carefully, he herded the cuttings into a small pile. There! He surveyed the patch of perfect park lawn with benevolence. Perhaps a break! He fumbled with the orange jumper sleeve, which at that moment was attempting to cut off the circulation in his wrist. Ten minutes after nine…

He tapped on the front of the watch. "How can that be?" he muttered to his rake. "Surely more time than…" He shook it. It was a watch with crystals and tiny batteries, and, though not expensive, horribly, certainly accurate. He wiped his brow, took up the rake, and began herding an errant leaf in the general direction of another errant leaf. Not wishing to go, it clung to some sympathetic grass. He began to dislike leaves. He wondered how many might make enough of a pile, enough to justify another rest.

"What are you doing?" asked a shrill little voice. A fat child with a ruddy red face and a skinned knee was observing him from just up the slope. The child was standing atop a rock twisting this way and that, and masticating a large wad of gum.

Mortie looked up. "Hi there, young man…!" he said.

"Hi there, young man," the child mimicked. Mortie, taken aback at this response, shaded his eyes to examine the child. "Well…" he said. "As you can see, I'm raking… It's…"

"Why…?" said the child. He blew a large bubble.

Mortie wiped his brow. His back had begun to ache, due to the tightness of his uniform, and he had been contemplating undoing the top half of his orange suit again. But somehow the notion of doing that in front of this child embarrassed him. He generally liked company at any time, but he wished this child would go away. One is supposed to like children. Anyway, he had been told that. An actual conversation with one was a mystery.

"Well, because… well, you see, son," began Mortie quite earnestly… "If you don't rake the park, the leaves will pile up and suffocate the…"

The kid twisted his face around and then blew a huge bubble, which collapsed on his face. "My Grammy says it's because you've been bad…."

"Uh, no… I'm…"

"Yes, you are…. *She* says you've robbed a bank or a gas station. You're a *jailboard or* something…. She says they let you out to work…"

"Well, well, what is this?" thought Mortie, staring at the child. His neck itched horribly. He fixed a cold gaze on the little delinquent. Well, well, well, what do we have here? It had been a while since he'd had close contact with children. The lens of time had softened his view of their species. He had forgotten; let down his guard. But here was one of them that he remembered. At least the enemy had declared himself.

"It's 'jail*bird*,' kid," he said brusquely. "Look, I'm a little busy here…"

But the child grinned, and having seated himself, twisted around, grinding his bottom into the rock, much in the manner of one absolutely certain of his safety, not to mention the fact that someone else would wash his clothes. "You look funny in that suit…," he said.

Mortie frowned and stood up straight, or as straight as the tight shouldered jumpsuit allowed. "I said I'm busy here, kid…. Do you mind…?"

"Like a great big tomato that ate too much…!" yelled the child, doing a little dance up on the rock and laughing loudly, a nasally sound, much like a defective drill.

Mortie pointed the handle of his rake at the child. "Look, kid…, I'm not really a parks worker… I'm … I'm a de*tec*tive…."

The kid stared at him in mock wonder… "Really?"

"Yes…" Mortie nodded, retreating into as much of a dignified posture as the tight jumpsuit would allow…. "Really… I'm on a stakeout. Now, if you don't mind…"

But the child stuck out his tongue…. You're not a *detective*…! You're a big, fat, pink jailboard….!"

Mortie started toward the kid, poking the rake in front of him. "All right, you little creep.... How'd you like to take a ride downtown with me... A little run into juvi...? Maybe some time with a big social worker matron. They like little delinquents... Ha, ha...!"

The child stuck his startlingly long red tongue out again and ran.... "You can't do anything to me, you cow...! Gramma...!" he shrieked as he ran... "A big, fat, pink man is trying to kill me with a rake... Grammmmaaaaaaaa!"

Using his rake as a cane, Mortie scrambled to the top of a steep, grassy bank. A knot of colorfully dressed ladies were there. They stared at him.

"Iiaaaaaaaaaaaaaaaaaaaaa...!" screamed the kid, rushing into their midst and disappearing behind their skirts. "He's trying to kill me, Gramma...!" In a few seconds, he peered out.

One of the women, dressed in a wildly flowery configuration, walked firmly up to Mortie.

"Shame on you, sir...!" she said. "Chasing a child..."

"Ma'am... I..."

She handed him a card. *Peace and Wellness Inc.,* it read.

"You need work on your Chakra."

Mortie nodded. "No doubt, ma'am..."

"Yoga will help...."

"Yes, ma'am," said Mortie.

"A calming tea, perhaps.... Good day, sir...." The group of ladies walked on. The child peered out from behind one of them and, seeing Mortie still watching, stuck out that huge red tongue at him.

Stewart Finkel, the park superintendent, had an office in the far back realm of the fairgrounds. The narrow road to his office wound around here and there, over potholes that someone had tried, without much effect, to erase with some grading and a very little gravel. Except for the whining of some machine, there was no sound. There were low, dilapidated buildings all around, but he could see no office. Finally, Mortie spotted a tiny, faded sign on a post that said *Office.* A barely visible path led a way through the grass around the back of one of the more dilapidated buildings.

It was hot and bright outside, and very gloomy and dank inside. With his eyes accustomed to the bright light outside, at first Mortie could not see the superintendent very well. In a few minutes, he was able to see a man who appeared to be a wizened older man with a pointy face – a very sharp face – a man who continually pursed his lips, the result of which was that, what with the dank and the gloomy, he looked like a rat.

"You threatened a child, Jablowsky?"

Mortie was still trying to see through the gloom. There was a musty smell. "It's Jablonsky…" he said. "And I didn't threaten anyone…."

"The whole Flower Power Garden Club saw you, Jablowsky… With a rake?"

"No…," said Mortie. "I mean, what they saw, sir, was… actually… 'Flower Power'?"

Finkel seemed bemused. "Yes…. It's some people who used to be in a sixties commune. Hippies…" On a hot day, you can locate them for a half mile by the patchouli smell, if you're down wind.

"They seem nice…"

"These are the ones who minded their investments," said Finkel. "They don't get together too often. Kind of a loose affair. Some of them, the ones who took a trip or two too many, have a little trouble remembering appointments. Their garden club motto is *Farm Out.*"

Mortie waited… uncomprehending.

"*Far out,* Jablonsky?" said Finkel, tapping out some words in the air. "It was a saying we had in the sixties. Right up there with *It's all good….*" *Farm out?* The sixties were a big deal…. We…"

"I was born in 1986," said Mortie, staring at a huge grandfather's clock standing in a corner. He liked clocks. This one was ticking loudly and insistently. "Nice clock…"

Finkel slowly turned his head in the manner of someone who has looked at something too many times. He stared at the clock for a few seconds.

"Katzman sent it here…."

"Oh?" said Mortie.

"Said he didn't like the ticking. You chased him… with a *rake,* Jablonsky…?"

"I was raking," Mortie said reasonably. "I forgot to put it down…." He nodded toward the clock. "Why didn't he just turn it off?"

Finkel said nothing. In the silence, the ticking grew louder, and then. "He drops in unannounced."

Then Mortie understood. "Katzman?"

Finkel nodded. "To make sure it's still working."

Mortie could now see a little better. He saw now that Finkel was a relatively young man. He could not resist venturing a question. He *was* a detective, after all.

"What did you do to…?"

"See… that's the thing," interrupted Finkel, reflexively running his fingers through his thinning hair, the remains of which had been strategically stretched and aligned along the ridge of his skull and carefully, with immense effort, knotted paintbrush-like, in a tiny pony-tail on the back of his scrawny neck. "I've got no idea… Probably it was some small thing. I've tried to sort it out…. Maybe it was nothing…." He nodded toward Mortie – actually more of a nose twitch than anything. "Do you think everything that happens has a reason…?"

Mortie shifted in his chair. "I don't know, sir…."

"Well, somewhere along the line I've learned that sometimes things happen…," said Finkel, smiling grimly. "And they happen no matter what you do."

He gestured generally toward the world beyond his gloomy office. "Take the financial mess in New York. One person says it's one thing, another says it's something else;

insists it's something else. You look into it. You look to find that one thing.... You don't find it.... The more you look, the less there is. There is no one thing that you can point at."

"I've never really thought about it that way...," said Mortie.

"You have *no* idea," said Finkel. "When I was first here, I thought it would help to be imaginative."

Mortie nodded, trying for enthusiasm. "Sounds good...!"

Katzman doesn't like imaginative people.

"Oh... I see...."

"Feels they might imagine being in his job."

"Ahh..."

Finkel tilted his head imperceptibly toward the clock again. "Sends someone once a quarter to check the workings." He lapsed into silence.

Mortie, normally an enthusiastic person, felt the weight of Finkel's office.

He nodded toward the door. "Perhaps I should just go...."

"I don't like this job, Jablonsky...," said Finkel.

Mortie's phone buzzed in his pocket, but he felt he should listen.

"I hate flowers."

"You do?" said Mortie. "Aren't you supposed to...? I mean, isn't it sort of a big part of your... job?"

"Hate 'em like death...," said Finkel. He made a sudden, abrupt, horizontal, chopping motion. "If it was up to me, I'd mow them all down and plant grass. Trimming, digging, weeding, weeding, digging. It's endless. "They make my allergies erupt like a volcano."

"So, what happened? The park seems great…."

"Yes, I know…. You think that when you're young… Oh, you always start out good. Ball of fire… Big ideas…. And then you're assigned to toilet duty. You ever wonder who cleans the toilets, Jablonsky?"

Mortie shook his head.

"We do…. And approximately ten seconds after you have to clean the diarrhea off the seat of an outhouse, your attitude toward people begins to change…. He sighed. "I did the right things…. Went to college…. I was big on campus. Opposed the war."

"Which war…?" said Mortie, without thinking.

Finkel gave him a sour look. "Vietnam, of course…. I marched."

"You marched? Well that's…"

"I did…. When we are young, we think it will all turn out. I did all the good things: spent a year in the Peace Corps… married a good girl I met there." He pointed at a picture of a somewhat squatty woman who was smiling ruefully out of a picture on a shelf. "That's Gloria…." I used to be a *people* person, Jablonsky," said Finkel. "I would tell people that, and I wasn't lying. I'm a *people person* I would say."

"And now…?" said Mortie.

Finkel smirked grimly. "I hate people. I hate parks... It's a giant exercise yard for every flasher, thong runner, paint-baller, and high grass blanket baller in the city; not to mention nocturnal grave diggers. And speaking of digging, don't get me started on the treasure hunters with their metal detectors digging holes everywhere..."

"I saw those!" exclaimed Mortie. "I thought it was badgers or something."

"I wish...," said Finkel. "Badgers, we could use. Plus, there's the back-to-nature religious groups."

"I had no idea...," said Mortie.

"Not the half of it," said Finkel. "You wouldn't believe it... Wiccans... Sunrise services up by Celtic Rock. Did you know there are self-appointed preachers who figure they have the right to sneak up to people who are innocently picnicking and scream at them...."

"Wow...," said Mortie. "A little extreme, isn't it?"

"Extreme?" said Finkel. "They're outright lunatics. I tell you, the zoo ain't got a thing over the parks.... So many holes, the place looks like Swiss cheese. And don't get me started on the suicides...!"

Mortie felt that he should change the subject. He pointed to some pictures of young people, a row of grinning, very happy, young people with their arms around each other, on his desk.

"Your kids?"

Finkel brightened. "Me.... And Gloria. I met her there... In Ghana. The two years I spent in the Peace Corps... It was great when I was your age. How could one go wrong with that, I ask you?

There was a large poster on one wall. Mortie peered through the gloom at it. Though it was somewhat faded, it showed a huge crowd of obviously miserable people huddled under blankets in the rain. They were apparently being harangued by some people from a stage. He pointed.

"Must have been satisfying dealing with disasters like that. Don't you find that they bring out the best in…?"

"That was Woodstock, Jablonsky….."

Mortie squinted…. "Oh wow, it is…!"

"I almost went…," said Finkel. "I was in New York. Some friends begged me to go." He held up two fingers an inch apart…. "I was this close."

Mortie was impressed. "What kept you away…?"

There are questions that shouldn't be asked; that instead should be left to complete their disintegration according to the law of unbroached questions. Finkel seemed startled somehow, as though Mortie's question had pried on a gear that wanted to stay rusted shut, or had unearthed something from a metaphorical graveyard that should have been left buried.

The clock kept ticking for a long while. "It was Gloria…," started Finkel. She… See, we were just married that time… And we'd just bought her parents' house…."

"Well *that's* good!" said Mortie.

"She wanted to go shopping that weekend. The *others* wanted to go… But she…"

Mortie waited for a moment. “So a bedroom set kept you away from Woodstock?”

Finkel’s phone began to ring loudly. He stared at it. “She liked that Southwest style then, she said…,” he said distractedly. “I don’t even remember what that is any more….”

“Mission…?”

The phone rang and rang. Mortie did not want to leave in the middle of a ringing phone. He stood waiting. Finally, the phone stopped ringing and the message light beeped frantically.

“Yes…. Mission…,” Finkel said, about the time the ringing stopped.

Mortie’s cell phone buzzed in his pocket.

Finkel looked up. “I was going to let you go, Jablonsky…”

Mortie’s face brightened.

“But I’m not.”

Mortie’s expression fell. “No?”

“You seem like a genuine person.”

“Oh, no, sir…,” Mortie started. “I’m not really that genuine. Not a parks type person either. If you wanted, I could…”

“So get out of here and…” Finkel smirked. “Make it fly….”

He punched the message button. There was an eeeeeeeee sound and a scratchy noise as from an ancient version of a phone recorder.

He waved Mortie toward the door. "And try not to kill any kids…."

Mortie started walking toward the door. A frantic voice could be heard. Something about a tree and…

"A body…?" said Finkel, rather more casually than one would expect. "Another hanger… eh?" He listened for a minute and then sat up straighter.

Mortie turned to listen.

"What do you mean, 'he was shot'?" said Finkel. "Have you called the police? What do you mean there's already one there? Who's Blackman?"

But by this time the orange suit lay on the floor. "He's my partner," said Mortie, who had fished out his wallet. He flipped it open and flashed his badge at Finkel.

Three

"I'd better get down there," said Mortie. He pulled open the door.

"Wait!" said Finkel. "I'm coming, too. I'll take care of my staff."

They bumped down the road. "I guess we're about to meet one guy for whom it wasn't all that great," said Mortie.

They bumped around a sharp corner on one of the park roads on the way down to the river. Nooky Glen," said Finkel

"What…?"

Finkel pointed down toward the river. "The high school students used to have art classes down here.

"Oh, that's nice," said Mortie, looking ahead.

"Then they figured out it was a nice isolated place for screwing."

They rounded a sharp little hill, dropped abruptly to the river, ran through a grove of trees and then doglegged back into a little valley with sharp, wooded sides, open toward the river. The land here rolled and was mostly wooded, overgrown with green poplar and maple trees. Thickets of dogwood lined the clearings.

Mortie could smell the river. "Pretty, here," he said. Two ambulances were at the scene. One was pulling away. Blackie was crouched by the body. His orange suit was draped on the fender of a squad. Another squad had pulled up and two officers were standing. A few park workers were watching from the road. Blackie was now sitting in the right seat of a squad, his feet on the running board, talking on his phone and squinting at a tiny computer on his lap. He waved at Mortie.

"Okay.... Okay.... You've got it?" he asked. "Okay... Okay.... Okay, that's good." He stuffed the cell into his pocket and began typing rapidly on the little computer.

"Over there..." he said, and gestured toward a tree tucked even further into the said.

"Dead?"

Blackie punched a button, paused for a second, and then unplugged the computer and stuffed it into a case.

"Yep, he's about as dead as it gets," he said cheerfully, for he was the sort of person who could not stand to see any animal injured or even an insect killed, yet could look at gunshot wounds and bodies all day.

Mortie gestured. "What's with the ambulance?

"It's for the guy who found the body," he said. "New employee... Wertsel, by name."

They were walking to the tree... "You talk to him?"

"Nope...," said Blackie. "He was not feeling too good. Said he was running some errand down here. Saw something over here. The body was dangling to one side, mostly on the other side of the tree." They were now at the body. "When he came around the tree, he found this..." Blackie grabbed the cover and peeled it back.

"Nasty, eh..." said Blackie... "Something of a shock, apparently. Had some sort of an attack...

"Any ID?

"Nothing. I cleared the area, took a picture, and emailed it to IT. Time is important, and so I took the liberty of scanning his prints, the labels of his clothing, and his shoes. Sent 'em all to IT. They'll start trying to ID the guy. Called the Morgue and Forensics."

Mortie nodded. "Good.... Anyone touch the body?"

"I don't think so...," said Blackie. "I called the super...."

Mortie looked at him. "So...?"

"He's sending Iverson to help us. Says to wait till he gets here."

"C. H. Iverson...?"

"That's who was available."

Mortie looked around. "Crapola.... Okay... Let's get everything done that we can before he gets here...."

A city vehicle came hurtling down the park road and skidded to a halt on the grass, leaving long skid marks. A short, thick man with opaque sunglasses got out and sauntered toward Mort and Blackie.

"What's the deal?"

Mortie gestured toward the tree. "Good morning, Lt. Iverson. The body is right there...."

"A hanger?"

"No, sir...," said Mortie. "The victim was tied to the..."

"Who cut him down...?"

"No one did," said Mortie. "He was just tied to the tree."

"*Just* tied?"

“Well… I meant…”

“Listen, Jablonsky…,” said Iverson loudly. “That was a citizen. A *person*. To be treated with respect….”

“We’ve followed every protocol, sir,” said Mortie. “All of the victim information that we could get without disturbing the body has been sent. What else do you want us to do?”

Iverson looked somewhat like a toad that might blow up. He went to the body, jerked back the body bag, and began fumbling around for the man’s wallet.

“There isn’t any ID,” said Blackie politely.

Iverson stood up and walked around, looking up as if he expected something to be hiding in the branches. He then stomped around, examining the grass. “Blackman, do you suppose you could notify the appropriate departments regarding this here victim…?”

“Done, sir….”

Iverson turned. “What do you mean, ‘Done’...?”

“Took a preliminary set of prints and sent them to the City and to the FBI, along with a photo,” said Blackie. “Scanned all of the tags on his clothes. Sent them to IT to get a head start. Time is important in these cases, don’t you think?”

“I don’t have to think…,” said Iverson. “And you think you’re qualified to…?”

“Oh good, I see the technicians have arrived,” said Blackie. A city vehicle was approaching.

“Hey look,” said Mortie, pointing at a couple who had just arrived in a sedan and a white van, and were now talking into some cameras. Their teeth flashed across the intervening space like little, white, iridescent signs. Mortie squinted at a sign on the white van.

BLOTO.., THE NEWS YOU CAN USE

“Wow…!” said Blackie, pointing. “*BLOTO” news*. Is that Missy and John? I love their show. They work so well together.”

“The News at Six. I hear they’re married,”

“The way they look at each other on TV, I’d say so…,” said Blackie. “How did they hear about this, I wonder?”

“They have a whole team to monitor communication…,” said Mortie. “They’re everywhere…. Just like movie stars.”

He and Blackie drifted over, trying to be professional. The two stars ignored everyone, recording introductory videos with the river as their backdrop.

“Hold still, will you?” Droaning barked at a young man who was trying to hold a mirror in front of his face. He smirked at a platinum blonde who was similarly employed, her mirror held by a replica of the other young man. “Way to go there, Missy.”

“What?” said Missy to her mirror. “God, it’s humid down here.” She pushed away the mirror. “What did you say?”

"I *said,* 'Way to go'... Nice stutter...."

"Stutter?" said Missy, glaring at him. "You should talk, Mr. Prissy pants."

"Oooooh...," said Droaning, clutching at his side. "I'm like... *so wounded.*"

"Well, if you ask me," said Missy, "Those pants make you look like a little girlie man." Her assistant finished touching up her hair as well as could be expected, under the circumstances. Missy nodded and her assistant, who might as well have been a piece of furniture, sprayed her hair with something from a can. "That's enough," she said, grimacing at the result. "This place is murder on my look."

"Your *look...?*" hissed Droaning. "Listen, Miss Bubbles, you're just jealous because I've got a better figure."

"Can it, girlie man...," said Missy, getting up and pushing the mirror away. She waved the others to get going. "We might just get the tape in the can before this guy rots."

"'Girlie man'...? Now you're stealing someone else's lines?" said Droaning smoothing his hair with his fingers. "Not for the first time, I might add."

"Right," said Missy. "My lines are no more fake than your teeth, bucky."

"Well, dear," said Droaning. "I can tell you one thing these pearlies have gotten me."

"What's that...?"

"A better contract."

Missy shot him a look of intense hatred. "You don't have a better contract."

"Ha," said Droaning. "I've seen yours…."

"You haven't seen *anything*."

"I *have* seen it…," said Droaning, complacently. "No comparison…. I make more, Missy."

"If you *have,"* said Missy. "There's going to be hell to…"

"Thirty seconds!" yelled someone.

"Camera one," said someone else loudly. A light came on. Instantly, Missy's expression became a focus of empathy and concern, followed by an intense, neon smile.

"John and I are here for *you* and you alone," she said to the camera.

"Yes," said Droaning, following her seamlessly, and gazing into her eyes with a look of concern mixed with adoration. "Yet another victim of violence in our city, this time in our sheltering green park. "Where, I ask you, is all of this going to end?"

Someone had propelled Lt. Iverson unceremoniously over to the two TV anchors and Droaning had shoved a microphone into his face. Iverson was alternately grinning idiotically at the camera, and gazing up at Missy, who, although not tall, was at least several inches taller than he.

"I don't know, John," said Missy sadly. "This is Lt. Iverson. Perhaps he can give us some insight into what is going on…"

"Paint us a picture of this awful event, Lieutenant," requested Droaning.

Iverson opened his mouth to speak, but before he could say a word, Missy interrupted him.

"Did you know the victim?"

This was such an unexpected question that Iverson was suddenly stage struck.

"Me…? No…! No, not me…," he stammered. "I was called in to take charge of the situation." He gestured toward Mort and Blackie. "They… These young men don't really have the experience. I mean, we all are concerned with…"

"Were drugs involved, Lieutenant?" asked Droaning.

"Drugs? I don't know," said Iverson, recovering a little, but still looking somewhat like a raccoon caught stealing garbage in the headlights of a car. "I would guess something like that…"

"There you have it, folks," interrupted Missy. "The scourge of drugs strikes again. Our nationally known police force on the job within minutes. Will they solve this one, John?"

"Only time will tell, Missy…," said Droaning. "Only time will tell."

"So remember, folks," she said. "We're on the news…"

"So you don't have to be," finished Droaning.

"That's it," yelled someone. "Wrap it…."

"Gotta move, people," yelled the man. "Fire down University…"

Iverson wandered off. Someone handed Missy a towel. She wiped her face a swipe or two, and tossed it on the ground. “Let’s get the hell out of this steam bath before I melt. And get my lawyer on the phone,” she yelled to a harassed looking young man as she strode toward a waiting car.

Four

The driveway to the Jablonsky estate ran for a half mile around small hills, through groves of elm and oak and aspen, down, down, across a wood bridge, over a brook and three fields, one of alfalfa, one a whitewashed horse paddock, finally straightening along a rolling pasture with white-faced Herefords, then up a long incline to the main house. The driveway was not asphalt, but instead was a ten foot bed of pebbles so that it seemed like a pale cream strip of ivory carpet through the green landscape. That had been his mother's idea, maintenance of it was someone else's… Bertram, her husband (now deceased, poor man), came up with the solution. Each year since he was six, Mortie and the local troop of Boy Scouts had spent a day raking the whole length of the driveway and pulling any weed that might have the effrontery to think of living within the path of the driveway. Of course bribery was involved; this day-long lark was followed by a picnic in the afternoon and a roaring bonfire and campout in the evening. A little soiree for forty or fifty guests kept the adults out of the way. This all was followed by a large donation to the Scout troop camping fund.

In the night, a downpour had drenched the hills and lightning had boomed, but now it was late morning and the sun was so hot that the warm air smelled of the five long flower gardens along the winding way, and Mortie drove with windows wide open. It had been two months since he had traveled this road. As soon as he turned onto the driveway and saw the flash of white in the distance that was the grand house… the house he had grown up in… the fields he'd roamed… a thrill, a familiar sense of exultation, filled him: *Home*. Then just as quickly… there was apprehension and a vague sense of unease.

Horace the butler greeted him at the door in khakis. He was also the head gardener, the manager of the vineyard, and would have been the cheesemaker, except that business had been given up years ago. He dried his hands while he considered Mortie. He smiled, a phenomena mostly visible in his eyes.

"Mortimer…," he said. "It has been too long…. I trust the world finds you well…."

"I'm fine, Horace…," Mortie said, his look taking in the living room and the east garden. "The gardens seem fine. How're things…?"

"Blooming, sir… blooming…. The rain gods have been good to us. The jonquils alone are worth a look if you…"

Mortie gestured toward the stairs. "Is she…?"

Horace nodded. "She is…."

"Mortimer…!" exclaimed Mrs. Constance Bertram Jablonsky, striding confidently across the gigantic parquet floored living room. There she was, tall, perfectly dressed, smiling, amused.., that light in her eyes. That look, that gentle light of love…, his enemy, his guilt maker, the source of that vague unease. Each time when he had been away he saw it anew. It had taken him his whole short life to recognize it, the look that reminded him of his mother's predilection for interference in other people's lives; interference that one often didn't know about until weeks or months after she had pulled on whichever strings she wanted…. She was sneaky. And she never…, ever was deterred.

Surely she wouldn't do *that*, he had thought time after time throughout his life.

Surely she *would.*

"My dear, dear Mortimer," said Mrs. Jablonsky. "How simply *wonderful* you've come to see your mother. I've been *so* worried for you these last days dealing with all of those…, those people down there in the city."

"You shouldn't call the Chief's office, mother."

"My dear," scoffed his mother, peering down her nose with amusement. "I practically got him his job. He's better off talking to me than those others." She cast him a knowing look. "I hear you've been busy…?"

"It was nothing…," said Mortie. "I can't stay long, Mother."

"Nonsense….!" she said, taking him by the arm and forcibly propelling him toward the kitchen. "You haven't been here for months! I'm dying to know.... Every little thing. Routing criminals with some sort of a machine. "

Mortie frowned. "Who told you about that? We weren't even directly involved. It was just..."

"Oh... someone I know heard about it.... And my friend Joan says there are bodies.... Tell me...! It's all over town! How exciting! I only wish Bertram were here," she said, trying to look downcast. She put her hand to her forehead. "Oh, if he could see how perfectly grandly you've performed."

"I've got something going, Mother. I have to..."

"You've just gotten here. I wouldn't *think* of it...," she said. "Milly is making a perfectly wonderful cold cucumber soup and some other good things, I'm sure.... She *so* wants to see you...."

She, *so* didn't. Millie the cook was, contrary to the gentle sound of her name, a skinny, morose, abrupt sort of woman who smoked like a chimney and swore like a... well, she really swore.... Why Mrs. Jablonsky had kept her, no one knew.

"Do you know how hard it is to get someone who can consistently make matzo ball soup that isn't too chicken-y?" she would say. "My god, and her omelets..." That probably wasn't all there was to it, but that's all anyone was going to get out of Mrs. Constance Bertram Jablonsky.

"Mortie...," his mother started, after they had been through the soup and into the very good watercress, spinach, and anchovy salad.

Mortie paused mid forkful. “What…?”

She was considering him. “Mortie…, do you think it would be okay for us to sell this place?”

Mortie stared in disbelief. “Sell it…?”

“Well… Not right away…. …” she said, putting a cool hand on his. “It’s just that I kept the place thinking you might find some nice person… and, well, you know, get married, start a family. But I barely live in one room, and the kitchen, and you don’t seem to be the marrying type… just now, that is….” Her voice trailed off sadly into silence.

“I’m not gay, Mother….”

“Oh, I don’t want you to think that I don’t understand. It’s perfectly fine with me, dear, if you are…. I’ve known any number of people in… in our little group who… who…”

Mortie sighed and dropped his fork…. “Mother… I’m not gay….”

“These nice people have been coming around with lots of money…. It would set us up for life. Wallengate says now is the best time…, you know, tax wise….”

Mortie got up…. “Mother, I have to go. Now, it’s your place. You can do anything with it. You know that.”

“I rattle around here so much now…,” she said. “And you know me. I need things to do.”

A tight feeling came back into his stomach. “Why don’t you find yourself some nice… person… to occupy yourself, Mother…? Mortie said. “You’re still young and… and beautiful….”

"Well, thank you, dear…." She looked at him steadily. "I know you think I was a little hard on your father…, on my Bertram…. But, really, he was the best…"

"A little hard…?" interrupted Mortie.

"Don't be rude, dear. We loved each other, dear…. I know you think I'm inclined to interfere in … things."

"You do…" said Mortie. "You've always done it. You can't help it."

"I most surely *don't* want to run people's lives," she said. "It's just that I do get a little bored. And most men…" She put her hand on his again. "Present company excluded, my dear, but most men are so dreadfully clumsy in… almost everything."

"I've got to get going…"

"Will you take Gloria Aschenhalt to the Police and Fireman's Charity Ball…?"

Mortie paused and then grimaced as one might remember something somewhat distasteful and possibly dangerous.

"So that's it…?" he said. "That's why you asked me out here?"

Mrs. Jablonsky smiled hugely. "Of *course* not… I merely thought it might be fun for you… "

"Anyway, isn't she in Europe?"

"She's home now…."

"Talk about a dangerous occupation…," he said. "Going out with Gloria Aschenhalt can be positively hazardous. If not for your reputation, then for your health. Remember the tar baby incident."

His mother laughed gaily. "Well, she was a child, dear...."

"Or the day my friend Birdy bet her she couldn't tie him up so he couldn't get loose."

"I don't recall that..."

"Well, she tied him to a tree."

"And...?" said his mother eagerly.

"Just plum forgot him there for a while."

"She *was* always good in Girl Scouts...."

"She went off for a few... hours."

"Oh dear. Was he hurt?"

"Oh no... Just a few mosquito bites."

"Well, that's good."

"A few hundred...."

"She got one of my friends to taste some mushrooms.... She was sure they were safe. He told me later that he wondered why she was looking at him so intently with those big innocent blue eyes. Thought she liked him."

His mother held a spoonful of soup almost to her lips. "This is so good...! Well, at least you remember something good about her...." She's just a little exuberant, dear."

"She's not my type, Mother...," he said. "My god, I'm not sure she's anyone's type.... Maybe some Martian."

"But she's very pretty...! And you haven't seen her for years."

"Well that's true... Wasn't she at some prison....?

"Shame on you!" said Mrs. Jablonsky, retreating across the expanse of the kitchen. She dropped some bread into a toaster and snapped the toaster lever down with a metallic 'kling!' "She was at finishing school. She was in *college.* A very prestigious one too."

"What is she doing, summer vacation…?"

"No," said his mother sadly. "She's been home working ever since her family lost most of their money."

"Lost their money…?"

"Yes…," said his mother. "Most of it, anyway…. They've sold their place and moved… To a rambler…. But…," she said, brightening. "She's back, now, and she's working at the hospital for the summer. I don't know what her job is, but my friend Gerty says she's studying something very exciting in college…."

"What is her major…?"

"Well, it's… Entomology… But…"

"Entomology…? Isn't that *bugs*, for god's sake?" said Mortie.

"She's very smart, I hear. She wants to be a *doctor*…."

"Doctor?" repeated Mortie, trying to reconcile his memory of Gloria Aschenhalt with being a doctor.

"Oh, come on, dear. The Prince of Wales went to the same school."

"Really…?" said Mortie.

Mrs. Jablonsky took a small bite of her dry toast. "Well, some prince, anyway. They're all about the same, I hear.

Please, Mortie…. Just this once, for me. I promised my friend Gerty I'd have you meet her, at least…"

They finished lunch, and after Mortie had gone to the kitchen to thank Millie for the wonderful luncheon soup (actually a little too tomato-y), he kissed his mother.

"I have to go, now…."

Mrs. Jablonsky suddenly looked very sad and small.

Mortie stopped halfway through the door. He sighed. "Okay. But if I do… Will you *stop*… what am I saying? Will you *try to restrain* your maneuvering around on my behalf? It isn't helping, you know…."

"My dear… I wouldn't *think* of interfering in your career…."

"Mother. You *would*… You *know* you would…. Anyway… I'll be there…."

"You're so wonderful!" his mother exclaimed, smiling. "Noonish, Wednesday, we're having a lunch at the Chrysopolis…. Thank you, dear…."

Five

The weekly staff meeting for the Criminal Division was held in the Ready Room. Officers talked general problems, and Captain Groatly, the supervisor of detectives, made announcements. Assignments were confirmed or announced; it was a relaxed, jocular assemblage, but still serious.

The Ready Room, known to the men as the Blue Room, was painted blue, and people who saw this room filled with blue coated patrol officers may have thought all this color the reason for the name. But the real reason was a bit of humor dating from the day a former police chief named Blighe (yes that's right) had been caught incoherently drunk and in a compromising position with a woman whose working sobriquet was "Bunny." In a bravado performance with his wife and several children gathered opaquely around him, he had shed a small river of tears, ardently begging for forgiveness. Alas, his performance wasn't enough, and he was forced out of his office. But thereafter, the room was referred to as the Blue Room in honor of his performance.

The defrocked chief did not exactly sneak off. Instead, feeling the psychic ground quake under him, he suddenly became an evangelical minister. He began preaching on street corners, a very scandalous eventuality, particularly to his former officers who encountered him there. From this beginning, he gained a small but fanatical following, and … and… being shocked, simply *shocked*, at the current tax structure, he had moved to Florida. There, he acquired an abandoned school for a church, a Mercedes, and a new wife: his friend Bunny. She, now having reformed and conservatively (but expensively) gowned, was also his secretary. Of course, all of this illustrates something… I'm just not sure what…. You figure it out.

Perhaps, it illustrates the circular nature of one's dharma.

Captain Groatly, the supervisor, a business-like man with grey hair, came bustling in, settled his papers on the podium, adjusted his glasses, and cleared his throat. Groatly held two degrees: one in sociology and another in criminology.

This did not keep him from talking as though he were back in Ward Six.

"Okay, here we goes tentionall gentlmens," he started, reading from the action sheet. "In the 31 foist block... sout, from der to abouts, oh 40 sometun, going over towad the riva…," he waved a sheet. "For youse that is workin' that area, youse can get onea deese that shows the perimeter of the focus area. Anyway…, ter's been a lotta auto heists in that area." He looked at the sheet. "Ten in the last six weeks… We tink itsa a chop-shop. I been getting a lotta heat from up top on dis…."

"Suspects…?" said a detective.

“Which teris a list of known perpetrators attached,” said Groatly. “Who’s workin’ that area?”

“Kilpatrick had been…,” said someone.

“Here’s da ting. Kilpatrick is out for this week. I repeets. Kilpatrick is out. Johnson’s is covering for him. Looteninent Overbight, is out too. He was workin’ chop for the last year. He’s up at Glenhollor getting dri…. ….. receivin’ … some medical care…. Now then, what wit dis err wictim in the pak we ain’t go’ no leeway. We were sho’t’anded befora dis anfortunate evint, what with waycations an all… The ree sult of which is that we is going to be ‘stremely shorthanded for da next tree wicks.”

Captain Groatly stacked some papers. “Now, this is what I got to do; I don’t want to do it – I don’t want to put the total burden on Mort and Blackie –

but I’m going to let them run with the body in the park for the time being.”

“Blackman can’t…!” somebody yelled. “He’s working a B and E wire job….”

The Captain held up his hand. “Okay, boise, that’s enough…. The ting abouts this is that we got the body in the park and … though I don’t really wanna have it did this way, I’m gonna let ‘em take it and run wit’ it….”

“Attaboy, Superman!” yelled someone.

“Wait! Wait,” said the Captain. “I’m sorry t’put the whole ting on youse guys, Mortie and Blackie, about the deceased down ter in god’s own green pak. But…” He held up his hand again. “I’m shur everybody will help t’boys wit’ dis ting if they calls for help, so's to make chur day isn't over tare heads.

"Can you believe those guys?" said Mortie as they were happily rushing out the door.

"Captain Groatly doesn't even have a cell phone…." laughed Blackie.

"He does, too."

"He does?"

"He can't remember how it works, so he doesn't bring it along." Mortie pointed toward the street. "Let's get out of here before they change their minds."

"That guy Johnson tried to impress me the other day..." said Blackie.

Mortie wheeled into traffic. "What?"

They hustled North down Central Ave. "He thinks Dire Straits is cutting edge music…."

"Hey," said Mortie. "I like Dire Straits…"

"So do I," said Blackie. "But … Oh, never mind." He was tapping information into his phone.

They had turned and were cruising slowly through a particularly seedy section of the city.

"Recalculating…," said a mellifluous voice from Blackie's GPS. "Turn right at the next intersection…."

"Where are we going?" Blackie asked, looking up.

"E. Q. Brown's place. If I can find him," said Mortie.

"Oh… did you know … ?"

"What," said Mortie.

"A name is coming through on the victim in the park."

"Well?" said Mortie.

"A guy named… get this… one Oscar Senevitch from … Residence Elm Street Apartments. West side of town. Wait… Texas… Assuming it's the same guy…"

Mortie was driving through a shabby, loosely developed neighborhood of old ramblers with bone dry lawns, weeds. Wild and dry brush grew everywhere.

Blackie looked up from his phone at the neighborhood. "This is where Brown lives?" Two hungry looking Shetland ponies and a burro peered at them from some sun faded sheds and a dusty corral behind the neighbor's house. "Yeah… this is about right for him."

"Somewhere, here," Mortie said. He slowed the car. "We're close… Here it is, I think."

Every fourth house had a car or truck up on jacks. Two men watched them. One hoisted a beer at them. Mortie nodded. The other started talking into a cell phone.

"They've made us," he said. He stopped in front of a ratty old rambler with a junkyard for its backyard. "Take the squad around to the back, will you?"

"You mean Elrod Q. Brown?" asked Blackie. "'Downtown Brown'? A runner, isn't he?" he added, sliding over into the driver's seat.

"That's right," said Mortie. "Runs like a roadrunner, if he can…."

Instead of the front door, he eased up the sidewalk and then to the side entrance of the house, where he could see part way back onto the street. An engine dangled from a huge hoist next to a garage so filled with car parts that there was one lane in and out of it. Piles of car parts occupied about an acre in the rear of the house. He knocked on the side door. No answer. He beat on the door.

"Brown…!" he yelled. "Downtown Brown. It's Lieutenant Jablonsky! We want to talk to you…!"

Out of the back of the house he caught a single quiet 'cling!' as from someone brushing against loose metal. He ran to the backyard in time to see a middle sized man sprinting down a lane between piles of crushed aluminum cans. The man disappeared through a back fence. There was a yell, then a crash…

"Got him!" yelled Blackie from behind the fence.

Mortie picked his way through the junkyard and squeezed painfully through the fence. A small man was on the ground, his face shoved into some high grass. Blackie was sitting on him.

"That you, Brown?" asked Mortie.

"It's me…"

"How come you always run?"

"Get your partner off of me!"

"We can take you in, you know… No running?"

"Okay, okay…."

Blackie stood up. He stared at Brown with disgust. Brown rolled over and sat up, rubbing his head. "Sheesh… You clowns! You didn't have to tackle me. I coulda been hurt…"

"We just wanted to talk, Brown," said Mortie. "Why do you keep running? It doesn't help your cause, you know."

"Instinct…" said Brown, looking up suspiciously. "What can I help you wit'?"

"A body, for starts," said Blackie.

"Where?" said Brown examining a fingernail.

"You know where…," said Mortie.

Brown shrugged. "I hear something about a guy in the park. Everybody hears something about a corpus delecti…. ina park… I don't know from nothin." He stood up. His eyes swiveled, taking them both in. He sneered. "I don't need to talk to you guys. Tink you so big now, you detectives. He pointed at his chest. "I'm clean as a whistle…." You got nada on me. That's wachu call Latin for n*ot*hin'…"

Mortie was staring at Brown.

"What's wichu?" said Brown.

"You know, Mr. Downtown," said Mortie. "Your hands are soft and clean as a baby's. That isn't right for someone who spends time around a junkyard."

"Automotive recycling center," said Brown with dignity. "The recycling of recoverable parts is a legitimate business, as you know. It's an *industry* and it's good forda environment…. So, if you guys don't mind…"

Blackie had been tapping on his phone.

"Gotta business license, Brown?" said Mortie.

"It's my cousin Alberto's…," said Brown. "It's a family affair…. He's got one…."

Blackie looked up from his phone. "Oh… Mr. Brown. It says here you missed a meeting with one Jesus Horeana Miranda, your parole officer. Says they want to have a little talk."

"That's a lie," blurted Brown, looking at the traitorous machine. "Look, Mortie…," he started.

Mortie stepped forward. "My name is 'Detective Jablonsky', to you. Or 'Sir'. Unless you want to really be Downtown Brown today."

"All right…! All right…!" said Brown, holding his hands up in a stop motion. "I got nothing on the dead guy…. Don't even know his name."

"It's Senevitch."

Brown looked blank. "What's a senevitch? Sounds like one of those diseases."

"Let's get him downtown," said Blackie, grabbing Brown by the arm. "We're wasting our…"

"There's just some talk," said Brown jerking away from Blackie.

"What talk…?"

"Notin' really… Just a lot of dope talk, you know." He shrugged. "It's always the same… Plenty of dope. Then nothing… Big drought, you know… Who knows…? There's not much crank on the streets. There's a lotta talk about everyone gettin' well again… People complain… A lot of marijuana around…" He pointed at his chest. "I don't use any crank. That'll kill you quick. There's been a new supplier on that. No hard stuff from them. There's some jaw about a turf thing. I don't know.... The outfit gets stiff-backed about anybody. I'm not telling tales here. Everybody knows it... I ain't no little tweety bird, Mor... Officer. Honestly...!"

They were getting into the squad. Blackie turned.

"How come they call you '*Downtown* Brown'?" he said.

Brown smiled hugely. "'Cause when I come to the plate with the ladies," he explained, "I always go all the *waaay* downtown... An' the ladies *luuve* me for it."

Brown disappeared through the fence.

"What exactly does a witch look like?" asked Blackie, punching furiously on his Blackberry, occasionally looking up and squinting around down the street as if one might fly by on a broom. He handed Mortie a newspaper and pointed to an article.

"Oh... I forgot.... Do you know this guy...?"

"Oh crap...," said Mortie, pulling over and scanning the newspaper article.

Fab Francine's Hot Rumors

A bust gone wrong - A demotion, a body!

What's this we hear? Something about a certain officer of the law – and not just any junior officer, but a scion of an old and reputedly wealthy family. This newly minted Lieutenant in our vaunted law enforcement ranks was, we are told, together with his partner, recently shunted and summarily ordered to don decrepit, smelly, orange suits, assigned to rake leaves in Parks!

Tailoring aside, we are informed by a heretofore unimpeachable source, that a picture of the officer enflagrante' insuitu, *is floating around like a large orange butterfly. A little birdie told me that this state of affairs came tumbling down as a result of an incident that included the drug task force and a botched raid that our two heroes came to the rescue in a most impolite and unpolice-like fashion with -- get this -- with the aid of a frontend loader!*

My sources tell me that not only is this true, but our upright burgomaster of the police force, our el numero uno *doesn't deny it.*

"We have no comment, except to say we never play favorites in our organization," Chief Powell fulminated, when confronted with this juicy tidbit. "Some of our officers are young and have to learn to abide by the rules. There is absolutely no favoritism in my force," he says.

But folks, there's more. It seems that these two can't stay away from trouble. Because, according to the same sources, they hadn't raked up enough leaves to make a pile when – you guessed it – a body showed up! They are now working that case, we hear, sans suits d'orange.

No clue as to whether the deceased is a victim of paaassion dahlings. Stay tuned.

"Who is it?" said Blackie.

"Francine Flambou…."

“Who…?”

Mortie grimaced. “He used to be Frank Flambou...”

Blackie looked up. “She’s a guy?”

“Was…” said Mortie, wheeling the squad onto Colfax. “Sex change…. Says she’s the person he was supposed to be.”

“You know him…?”

Chatter suddenly on the radio. A fire on the north end of town. Traffic talk. Mortie turned to bypass it.

“Her…. Ought to… I graduated with him. She was a *he* then…. Played on the tennis team with him.”

“Oh,” said Blackie who resumed tapping on his Blackberry. He suddenly stopped and stared at Mortie.

“What,” said Mortie feeling Blackie’s glance.

“Nothing…. Where to, now?

“To meet a witch?”

“We’re going to meet a witch…?” He stared at the phone. “Which type…?”

“What do you mean, ‘which type?’” asked Mortie, turning onto 4th Avenue and heading north.

“Well, there are all sorts,” said Blackie. “Did you know that the word “witch” comes from the Anglo-Saxon word *Wicca…?*”

“What?”

“It meant something like a magician who is *against* the power of evil…. And basically it was a female thing originally related to fertility….”

Mortie was thinking of Gloria; blue, blue eyes, stringy, gangly, always loping along like a colt, always joking, but with an acid, ice-pick wit when she wanted. "So…?"

"So, they were sort of the tribal healers and wise people…"

"What happened?"

Blackie tapped furiously for a while… "Do you want the short or the long version…?"

"The short version…."

"The church saw witches, or the "Old Religion" as a threat, and began persecuting them."

"Persecuting?"

"Torture, water boarding, dunking, killing…"

"Oh….."

"Uh huh…. The Inquisition began in the 1200's. After that, everyone got in on it. Did you know that in France in the late 1600's over 30,000 people were executed during the reign of Henry III?"

Mortie had slowed and was peering at some addresses. He grimaced. "Why would I know that?"

"People were encouraged to inform on each other. If you denied it, you were obviously guilty…." Blackie was still looking at his phone. "There are various types of witches, according to this…. "Oh, nothing…," said Blackie. "Listen to this: Apparently the idea of broom flying was a misinterpretation of a pre-Christian ritual in which the women rode their brooms into the celebrations."

Mortie drove, squinting at the building numbers in the bright sunlight. They were far down University Avenue, next to some high tech manufacturing, and the University. College students with backpacks, or on expensive looking bikes. Small gaggles of harried looking office workers hurried along the streets, at least Mortie hadn't seen any large gaggles, and he was in fact still peering at the building numbers. "That's interesting," he said after a moment. Witches weren't the least bit interesting to him. He squinted again. "Who is this we're going to see?"

"It's her," said Blackie enthusiastically. "The Wicca…. The witch… She's a witch!"

"And why is this important?"

"Well…," started Blackie. "It's … It's pertinent to…"

"Never mind," said Mortie, looking over at him. "You just wanted to meet one, didn't you?" He peered more. "It's here somewhere…. Why can't they make these numbers bigger?"

"You're one hundred feet away…," said Blackie, looking at his phone.

They pulled up to an address, a very snug looking little place, a coffee shop with bright fresh flowers on each of the ten or so tables. Several people were sipping coffee and pecking away on laptops.

Mortie gratefully ordered a coffee from a tiny young woman with perfect teeth and chocolate hair, and a horribly chirpy voice that grated on him. Blackie, however, seemed stricken. When the dark haired woman smiled at him, he seemed unable to talk.

Mortie showed his badge. “Is Mrs. Perlsworth here?”

“She’s due back any minute.... I’m Cerise....”

Mortie sipped his coffee. Blackie pecked on the keyboard of his tiny laptop. A woman came over.

Mortie could not help staring. Mrs. Perlsworth was about forty years old; and beautiful, with the faintest hint of corrosion about her, an intriguing corrosion like a ripe, beautiful fruit that is perhaps a little past the peak of its sweetness. She smiled at him, a curiously vulnerable smile that said, “I was once a beautiful child and now I’ve seen all that you can send me.” It was a bemused smile, a knowing smile.

“It’s not the tables on the sidewalk again, is it?” she asked. She smelled wonderful. “I knew zoning didn’t like that many tables, but I didn’t think they’d send the police....”

“No... No ma’am...,” blurted Mortie, who had stood and pulled out a seat. She sat down. He tried not to stare. “No... Nothing like that....”

She laughed. “In that case...” She extended her hand. “I’m Melissa.”

“We understand you’re a ... a ...” he began. “That you’re in the park frequently? We’re investigating an offense that occurred there and were running down any and all people who were known to be in the park frequently to see if they might have seen anything out of the ordinary… in your um… services. That is, we…"

A light of humor grew in her eyes. "You're asking a Wiccan if they've seen anything out of the ordinary?" she mused. "Do you mean something about the body we've been hearing about?"

Mortie nodded. "Do you get a lot of people at your um… your services…?"

She shrugged. "It varies… Not everyone makes all of our gatherings… Wiccans have twelve or thirteen full moon celebrations each year, usually, although everyone tries to get to four of our services, the ones that were most important in what we call the Old Religion."

"What would they be?" asked Blackie.

"They are the two annual equinoxes, the point in the year when there is half daylight and half darkness and the solstices when the days are the longest. Lots come out to *Litha* …"

"Litha…?" said Mortie, who could not decide whether this was interesting, or just that he liked looking at her…

She nodded. "Yes. The summer solstice, which is in June, when the sun is highest and the day the longest. Fall is a big one, too. *Mabon* in late September is a popular celebration. It is the fall equinox, a day of equal light and dark.." Mortie had a hard time taking his eyes off her. He had the sinking helpless feeling that if he looked very long into those eyes he would want to hand himself to her on a platter.

"Do you have a list of your people who come to these gatherings?" asked Blackie.

She considered Blackie. He stared back opaquely, not seemingly affected by her beauty in the least.

"We do not," she said. "Anyone with a good heart is welcome to our services."

"Ma'am…," said Mortie, handing her a card. "I hope that if you think of anyone, or any circumstances that might bear on this, you will call me or Officer Blackman. A homicide has happened. A very vicious homicide. If you want the park to be a safe place, I hope you will help us."

"Of course," she said, getting up. He smelled her as she passed.

"Is that a Blackberry?!" exclaimed Cerise, coming over. She brought out hers and soon Blackie was explaining some arcane element of its use."

Mortie finished his coffee. He coughed. Cerise and Blackie were laughing and giggling and pointing at something on one of the Blackberries.

"Officer Blackman," he said.

Blackie suddenly jumped to his feet. "I have to be going…!" he said, a stricken look on his face.

"Bye, bye," waved Cerise to Blackie.

"I think you've found a friend," Mortie said dryly as they wove in and out of traffic.

Blackie flushed an unhealthy red color.

They drove in silence for a while.

"Want to meet for breakfast?" asked Blackie as they were approaching their office. "And then go from there?"

"I can't. I've got Abby Roedes."

Blackie shook his head. "You're still doing that? Can't you just play squash or lift weights…?"

Mortie nodded a little sheepishly. "It's a good workout."

One day, his mother had handed him a certificate.

Exercise Your Prerogative! Introductory Offer! Abby Roedes Dance, Traditional and Modern, Aerobic Workouts!

"You are a policeman, dear," his mother had said. "You have to stay in condition. You don't want to be one of those awful pot-bellied, donut dunking patrolman I see hanging around that awful Dunkin Donuts over on Franklin…. I signed you up for a workout…."

Abby Roedes, a dear friend of his mother… one of her hundreds of dear friends… had once been fat. Flabby Abby, classmates had cruelly referred to her. Many, however, are the uses of adversity. With a couple of divorce settlements to raise enough capital to lease a building (her last husband, a lawyer, had helped her with the legal parts) and to get going, a good dietician and an iron discipline, she turned herself into a diminutive knot of spiky haired, brightly dressed, smiling muscle, and the proprietress of Abby Roede's Dance Studio.

“A dance studio? Ma, I can’t go to a dance studio. I’d never hear the end of it.”

“Nonsense....”

“And, by the way,” he added, partially to quell the sudden drooling desire for a nice hot, fresh donut. “What were you doing over on Franklin?”

“Don’t change the subject,” she said, though she herself changed the subject constantly. “And try not to be obstinate. Just give it a try.”

“I thought you wouldn’t be caught dead in that part of town.”

“Oh, I don’t know,” she said waving vaguely. “It’s a nice change. There’s an Egyptian restaurant there and a Thai place. Good food ... Cheap, too. Look,” she said. “Just go. She’s my friend. There are lots of nice girls there, Mortimer.”

“They consume their children, Mother.”

He went to the workout. Apparently, she had missed her calling as a sadistic drill sergeant. An hour later, a quivering mass of rubber muscles, he staggered out the door, surrounded by the still cheerful ladies who did not seem at all quivering or staggering.

“See you Thursday, Mortie!” Abby Roedes had yelled. “You did great!”

It was getting late. The traffic on Rockwell was heavy. Mortie was a good, but impatient driver, weaving in and out of traffic. “Everyone else lifts weights and you go dancing,” Blackie said, looking ahead.

"You'd change your mind if you did it..."

Mortie never saw the truck coming.

"Look out!" Blackie yelled.

Mortie could not figure out where he was. An angel was staring down at him and was shining a light into his eyes. His head felt like his brain was slopping around inside, like a bowl of aching pudding.

"Mortie...?" the angel was saying. "Oh good, you're coming around."

He drifted. It was a boat. It was rocking, and he felt a little sick. He was in a boat at uncle Felix's that summer up on the lake.

"We'd better tie up and go in," Uncle Felix was saying. "I'll crank the siren. I think the wind is up." A siren. An accident. He tried to sit up, but the angel pushed him down.

"Just lay there, Mortie," the angel said more brusquely than an angel should. "Don't move. You've been in an accident. We have to get you to the hospital for a little check. Nothing wrong, I think, but a nasty knock on the head. All things considering, it could have been worse."

That voice seemed familiar. He tried to focus on the angel. He suddenly recognized that wild tangle of reddish blond hair. A sudden panic. Oh god. It was Gloria.

He groaned and sat up. "Hello, Aschenhult..." he said. "I heard you were a doctor or something. How could it have been worse?"

She pushed him down. "It could have been me, you idiot," she said. "Now stay put! You've had a concussion. And I'm not a doctor yet. I'm a paramedic…."

"Blackie…?"

"He's fine…," she said. "He's seeing to your car…. That truck hit your side and you hit your head…."

He felt around for his phone. "I'm fine…. Got to get back…"

"I've got it," she said.

"Well, give it to me," said Mortie irritably. Talk made his head hurt.

"You'll get it."

"I'll get it? It's mine, Aschenhult. Now…."

"After the scan, Mortie. We've got to see if there's any damage in there. I doubt it, but people have died from this."

"Forget it," he said. "Give me my phone." He felt around… "Where's my weapon, for god's sake?"

Gloria sighed. "Your partner's got it," she said. "Mortie, you always were thick headed and stubborn. And you haven't changed a bit. If I give it to you, will you just get the scan?"

"Fine, fine," he said, feeling very abused by her manner, besides the fact that his head ached and he was vaguely nauseous. But after calling Blackie, who said he was on his way, he felt better. He refused to be wheeled into the emergency room, but when he stood up to walk in, his legs turned to water. He grabbed for her shoulder.

“I’m fine…,” he said, leaning heavily on her, stumbling once, so that they almost fell over.

“You’re fine, all right,” said Gloria. An orderly came over…. He was smiling.

“Well, what have we here…?”

“A cop,” Gloria said. “A dumb cop…,” she added, shoving him, rather roughly, he thought, into a chair.

“Well, one thing’s for certain,” he said, grateful to be sitting upright.

“What?” she said. She was typing something into a monitor that had been wheeled up to them.

“Growing up hasn’t improved your attitude.”

“I took this job to help poor people,” she said, tapping away at the keyboard. “People who need it. Not rich little boys playing at cops.”

“I’m not…”

“There,” she interrupted, making a few more entries. “A nice orderly will take you for a picture of your head. Not that I expect them to find anything. But you can never tell. See you at the Chrysopolis, Mortie.”

She walked off without looking back.

Blackie showed up in an hour. Mortie wobbled out of the entrance and into the car. They sat for a moment. Blackie considered him.

“You okay…? I’m not sure that you ought to be out of there. Mortie, you should let them do what they do best. This is a pretty good hospital.”

"Of course I'm okay," said Mortie impatiently, although the world seemed to be slightly fuzzy and the sun was scaldingly bright. He was sweating a little.

"What did the scan say?"

"It said I'm fine...," lied Mortie, who had no idea what it said. "Drive carefully. I don't know if I can take another collision today. Did you get all of the parks people?"

"I did. I got a list from Jacobs and ran backgrounds on all of them."

"Full and part-timers?"

"All that I could. There might be more. He keeps a floating group, but I think I got everyone except a couple."

"And...?"

"And not much. A few minor things. Most of those guys are just trying to make a buck. One guy had two dope beefs."

"When?"

"Years ago.... Nothing new. He did sixty days in the Brownville jail. No picnic. That's about it. Been clean since. Not one of them had anything violent except two who had domestic charges, both dropped. The only common thread, if it is one, is that half of them are from Texas."

"Texas?"

"Yes. Probably some of them, or most of them, are undocumented."

"Par for the course... Anything more on the deceased?"

“Still running it down,” said Blackie, weaving slowly through traffic. He shot a glance at Mortie. “Would some food help?”

At the thought of food Mortie had a spasm of nausea. “No… Water, maybe.”

Blackie got into the car after getting two bottles of water at a convenience store. “It’s a strange thing about the body,” he said.

“Why?”

“Because his clothes were wet.”

“So…?” said Mortie, drinking some of the water and pausing to ascertain the effect. He felt a little better and so drank a little more. “He was dragged up to the tree in the night… Dew…”

“He was muddy, too,” said Blackie.

“Oh… Is…?”

“Forensics is running tests and Weisman’s office at the Morgue is doing the autopsy and the rest.”

Mortie pointed. “Let’s go there now.”

Weisman dealt with dead people all day, and was thus a jolly cherubic man who seemed to be always bustling around happily. On his wall was a diploma from Harvard Medical School.

“We were just passing by…,” said Mortie.

“And you want the dope on the dead guy in the park,” said Weisman, hustling around his office humming Wagner and stacking papers here and there. He began typing something into a computer.

"Uh… Yes, sir," said Blackie.

"Nothing definitive yet. Tests aren't done." He looked up. "And the last time I said something, somebody acted on it, and that didn't turn out so good. So then they tried to lay it on me."

"Nothing?" said Mortie. "We aren't going to hold you to it."

"Well," said Weisman after a long pause. "I don't think the bullets did much to him."

"No?" said Blackie.

"No… I think he drowned," said Weisman.

"Not shot…?" asked Mortie.

"No… He was shot…. But that's probably not what killed him."

"How do you know that?"

"I peeked," said Weisman. He giggled, a sound which caused Blackie to slide his chair back a few inches. He gestured wildly. "We have to run tests… Fantastically insightful tests! Science at its best!" He grimaced. "We'll know in a few days…."

He stared at Mortie and then produced an instrument with a little light on it.

Mortie tried to stop him. "Look, we have to get…"

"Quiet… I hear about some accident."

"I'll be outside," said Blackie…."

Weisman ignored him and began peering into Mortie's eyes with the light. "I know your mother. A fine woman. This will take nothing… I never get to work on live people.

Just let me do this, Lieutenant Jablonsky. I'm still a doctor…."

The light bored into Mortie's eyes. He winced. Weisman sat back down.

"How long until you're off?" Weisman asked, scribbling out a prescription.

"Not long."

"I think you'll be fine, but you need to sleep. Here…," he slid the prescription across the desk. "If you have headaches. Get these."

Outside, Mortie crumpled the prescription into his pocket.

Blackie was waiting. He pointed at his Blackberry. "Tookie from IT sent us this. Senevitch had a job. A box company. Here's his address.

"Okay," said Mortie. "I'll go there. You start on the parks workers. Pull the basics on everyone down there."

Six

In her eyes, burned the eager light of a zealot - a box zealot. Joyce McAdams, the president of Universal Boxes Inc., was a short, ruddy-faced woman, who scuttled into the lobby, extending her hand from some distance away, shaking Mortie's with a vigor that caused a drone of pain to roll through his head.

"There'll always be boxes!" she said. "Boxes are our lives!"

"Oh…?" said Mortie, not really knowing what else to say.

A sign on a wall read;

UniBox Inc. - Don't Ma e a Move Without Us!

Mortie had been staring at the sign. Someone had removed the *k* and it had not been replaced. This bothered him. He felt woozy. Why would they do this? Who knew these things? The world was filled with unknowable phenomena. Perhaps the man had a secret animus against *k*'s. Perhaps he was an existential painter, an artist. Or… a failed writer! If the sign still communicated the idea, was it wrong to remove the *k*? Perhaps vowels were next…. Mortie shook his head, causing a gentle wave of nausea to break over him.

Mrs. McAdams waved a finger in an ecstatic undulating motion, causing Mortie's stomach to undulate weirdly. "Yes, yes, yes! …" she said, practically giving off steam in her enthusiasm, and nodding so eagerly that for a moment Mortie had an insane vision of her head coming unhinged and rolling across the floor. "Yes, always…! We here at UniBoxes love boxes. Your corrugated cardboard box is a thing of beauty. A thing of art!"

Universal Boxes Inc., a dilapidated brownstone far out on the west end in an area of rolling oak covered hills, had the pleasant smell of the inside of a cardboard box. Except for the distant whir and soft clatter of machinery, it was a quiet place, one of those places that you know has stayed exactly the same from the day that it was built. You also know one of these days this place would be shut, the victim of modern economic theory, which states that if you can employ some person in another country at a dollar an hour, why pay ten dollars?

And then, after the employees are done standing around, wondering where their jobs have gone, and after some politicians show up at the wake, using words like "*proactive*" or "exciting" or "*opportunities*" or perhaps "*public/private partnership*", or maybe *retraining*… which means qualifying you to work for some fast food establishment… all of which mean you are about to get screwed. Then the building would become forlornly empty, and then if it is lucky, a neighborhood center, then a bicycle shop, then a coffee house, and finally, when the plumbing and the heating and the roof fail, it will become the object of a bulldozer, the site eventually turning into some very ugly townhouses. And furthermore … Ooops … I do apologize profusely. That opinion isn't needed here, and that sorrowful tale hadn't actually happened yet to Universal Boxes Inc..

"Beautiful and useful!" she said. "Think of it…." She raised a finger toward a faded yellow ceiling. "Without boxes, nothing could be done. Commerce couldn't happen. Fruit couldn't be shipped. It'd rot! Rot! The modern box was developed in America the Great in the 1890's. No modern war could take place without your cardboard box. Isn't that wonderful? Think about it!"

"It would seem a shame…," said Mortie vaguely.

"It's strong, too…. It's very strong for its weight. They've made shelters of it. Bums sleep in refrigerator boxes. They love 'em!" she shouted.

"You've been here a long time?" said Mortie partly to quell a sudden aching in his head at being the brunt of her enthusiasm. He looked at the shabby building.

McAdams nodded. "We're about the only company left that hasn't moved to China."

"What about plastic?" said Mortie. "Bubble wrap, and that sort of thing."

This apparently was not the correct thing to say to a corrugated cardboard box person. Her countenance soured. "Yes, alright…," she said, waving vaguely… "Yes, well, new technology is always entering the field. We here at UniBoxes embrace change."

She seemed to see him for the first time. "What can I do for you? Oh yes, Senevitch. We heard.... Really, too bad. We here at UniBoxes feel for his family...."

"He worked for you?"

She nodded.

"How long?" he asked. "Months...? Years...?"

"Ummmm. I'd have to look," she said. "I think... Hmmmm... Three years... almost. A good worker. He missed some work, but he always made it up. Some of the time he'd work like hell. He'd be a ball of fire."

"And then...?"

"And then sometimes you'd catch him sitting there like he wanted to disappear from the world."

"Did he drink or do drugs?"

She laughed. "This is a box factory, it ain't a social service. But we're not big. If they do drugs a lot, someone here would know. So, I doubt it. If they show up and work diligently, we don't ask them what they do in their spare time. We sell all over the country," she said proudly. "You make it, we box it."

"May I see his employment file?"

She hesitated. "Do I have to...?"

"No," said Mortie. "We can get a search warrant, but I don't see any need for that yet. It would be a convenience."

"Is that all?"

"For now...."

"Caskets have been made of it!" McAdams said as she handed him a file. "They're beautiful!" She stopped and turned around. "Planters for plants you can stick right in the ground! Cremation ash containers!" she shouted.

Mortie retreated to a desk, scanning Senevitch's file. Home address was different from the one given. He had moved recently. Social Security number. Divorced, a daughter and a son. He tried to scan quickly. He suddenly felt queasy again. He stopped at a fountain that looked as if it hadn't been used for years, ran the water for a while, and then drank some of the flat tasting, chlorinated water. He sighed, trying to get a handle on Senevitch's life. Not great. Not the worst. Forty-nine years old. Working in a box factory. Not much of a life…. Back to the report. A complaint to accounting, and a minor accident. A minor accident with a forklift. Commended in the last several years for working after hours.

He drove home. Slowly. He felt light-headed and it was getting dark. Oncoming headlights hurt. His cell rang.

"Wait a sec. I…" he said. He pulled into a turnout. "Okay… give it to me."

"You don't sound good," said Blackie.

"I'm all right." He felt around until he found his bottle of water. He drank some of it and closed his eyes.

"I've run background checks on all of the workers. About the same as before. Except I don't believe them."

"Why?"

"I don't know," said Blackie. "I think there are more people. Remember when we were working?"

"That wasn't work. That was slavery," shuddered Mortie.

"Well, the total doesn't come up to the number of guys I saw. You know I have a habit. I..."

"I know you count. Anything and everything," said Mortie. He opened the door and vomited on the street.

"What was that?" said Blackie.

"A bad oyster," said Mortie.

"Mortie... that isn't funny. You'd better get home. Or to the hospital...."

Mortie washed out his mouth and spit out the door. "What about the count?"

"I think there's more people around there. But I'm not sure. And one more thing..."

"What's that?"

"The truck that hit us was stolen...."

"So...?"

"So... I think somebody doesn't like us around the park."

"We should get over to Senevitch's place and start running down his friends."

"We can't tonight. We have to see the Super."

"When...?"

"Eleven in the morning."

"Oh...," said Mortie, grateful that it would be late.

Mortie's apartment was on the third floor of a rehabilitated flour mill. It was a loft, a large room with a balcony that overlooked the river. On one end of the loft was a large bed. The walls were thick concrete. It was a very quiet place. He staggered up the stairs, put on a Mozart CD, and tried to eat some food. He turned down the lights and lay on the couch. He closed his eyes. Peace. A ringing. He swam up to consciousness.

His phone. He had forgotten to turn it off.

"Mortie…!" said a deep female voice.

At first, he could not figure out who it could be. "Francine…?"

"Of course, dear. Who'd you think sounds like me…?"

"Look Francine, could I get back to you…?"

A pause. "You don't sound too good, Mortie. Anything wrong…? I heard something about an accident…."

"Francine… Where do you get this stuff…?"

"I have people everywhere, daahling…."

"Look… It's nothing… I'll call you back in the morning…?"

"Bye, sweetie…."

He drank some water, turned off the phone, and crawled into bed. In the night, he woke up from a dream in which Gloria was a Wiccan who couldn't get her broom started in the morning. Late in the night, when the western trains blew their approach to the cities, he woke. He was very thirsty. He swished water around, spit it out. He drank and drank. He crawled back in bed.

The phone was ringing. The sun was shining. Nine o'clock. It was Blackie.

"How are you?"

"Fine…."

"I've got Senevitch's home address. And we've got the Supp... at eleven."

He showered and shaved and was out of the door in an hour. He felt better…, a lot better.

The bright red neon of Hassan's Hot Coffee kiosk caught his eye.

"Officer Mortimer!" yelled Hassan from inside his kiosk. "You honor me… What may I do for you, my friend…?!"

"One I Bomb," Mortie said out the window. "How's business…?"

Terrible…," said Hassan sorrowfully, bustling around to woosh out the Istanbul Bomb. "I shall go broke soon… My children…"

"Go to the best private schools," said Mortie. "And you own an apartment building…."

"But the renters…. There is no richness…."

Captain Groatly's office was time warp, a monument to the 1950's. Mort and Blackie perched like puppets on a high, hard sofa with the plastic still on it. Between the sofa and the good Captain's desk was a laminated imitation wood coffee table upon which were some very lifelike plastic flowers. Mortie felt that he recognized several poppies. An almond-colored refrigerator stood in a corner. A huge, signed photograph of Eisenhower smiled benignly on all this from a beige wall next to some garishly bad abstract art confections. Mortie, who loved art, stared at them.

"Ah…, now look, boise," said Groatly, looking concerned. "This guy in the park. I hopes you runs down this guy quick. I would tink it don't look like much anaway and we got a lot to do. It looks like a soo-acide, don't-it…? We might have to takes youse guys offa dat for a day or two to take up a stakeout, 'cause Billy Overbight is up at Glennholler getting his everyother yea dryout…. I don' know how long we can cover for William…. I know his partner Frank was killed and he's got a couple a other issues, but…. He's a good officer, but he's about run da string out, tho' I must say so far's I know, he's never flew his aeroplane under da inflence, if you know wat I's means…."

"How is it going with Billy?" asked Blackie, who was a friend of Overbight.

"Touch and go… Touch and go," said the Captain.

They talked for a while. Captain Groatly seemed satisfied.

They were hustling down the street after the meeting. "Do you think that Captain Groatly might actually have a sense of humor?"

"Why?" asked Blackie.

The manager of the Elm Street Apartments was a tiny woman who alternated easily between cheesy, cloying warmth and an avid, troll-like interest in her company's money.

"I d'nno about this…," she said, walking ahead of them toward Senevitch's apartment. "I haven't seen his relatives. Not hide nor hair, as they say…. I coulda rented it by now. I'm losing my shirt on that place if I can't collect the rent."

"So you own these apartments," said Blackie.

She scowled at him and fumbled at her belt. "Yeah… And you're a comedian. I wish… Let's see. Damn it… Keys for everything…." She inserted a key in the door, wiggled it, and tried another. The latch clicked and the door opened. "What's going to happen to his stuff?"

"I'm sure someone will come forth to…" started Blackie.

"I'm sure they *won't*…," she said, gesturing them into Senevitch's apartment.

"Nice place," said Blackie, looking around at the plush décor. He wrinkled his nose. "A smoker…"

Alice, the manager, frowned. "Smokers…. Cost us every time they leave. We have to clean everything. The drapes, alone… You wouldn't believe it…."

"Where is the computer," asked Blackie, pointing to a small table next to a book case.

The manager shrugged. "I don't know…."

"The charging cord and mouse are here and the LED screen, but the hard drive is gone…," Blackie said. "Who's been in here?"

"No one...," she said. "Though, there's a hundred apartments here. I can't watch everyone who comes and goes."

"Do you have security cameras?"

She nodded. "That, we do.... We pride ourselves on being a safe place."

Blackie was sorting through some neat stacks of CD's on the book case. One was labeled *backup files*. Empty.

Mortie was in the kitchen. A small basket on the kitchen counter held a small pile of match books. He found a paper towel and used it to sort through them without touching anything. He found a plastic bag in a drawer, looked around to make sure the manager wasn't watching, picked up four of them with a fork, put them in the plastic bag, and stuck it in his pocket.

"How long did he live here?" he asked.

"Not long...," the manager said, from a station by the entryway door. "Really, he was a very nice man, at least as far as the times I met him. Quiet. He was almost the perfect renter. Except for the smoking, that is. Always brought the rent in on time.... Never had any noise complaints. He seemed to go out of his way to be a quiet person."

"They aren't all like that, are they?" said Mortie.

"You wouldn't believe what some people think they can do in an apartment...."

"Like what...?" asked Blackie, who came into the kitchen.

"Like the very nice couple who used the dish washer to wash diapers…."

Mortie stopped and stared at her. "Didn't they have a clothes washer…?"

She smiled wanly. "Said it was broken…. Said it was our fault…. It turned out they'd been washing used motorcycle parts in there…."

The tiny manager was looking around at the apartment.

"I suppose I could get that woman…"

"What woman?" asked Blackie.

She looked around warily. "That woman who gets rid of ghosts…"

Mrs. Jablonsky's black Cadillac slid slowly down Broadway. "I could have gotten a cab," Mortie said. "I'm just picking up my car."

"Nonsense…," she said. "We don't spend any time together."

"Mother…?"

The tone of his voice made her turn to him.

"Yes…?"

"Why is it," he started, "that the people who came … of age in the 1960's seem to … Well, I don't know what it is … But it's like they can't seem to get past their experiences of that time…." He was silent. "I mean, they remind me of some child who can only remember some favorite Christmas party or something…." He groped for some words to describe the feeling he had. "You were there…. I mean, I know you weren't a hippy or that sort of thing, but…."

Mrs. Jablonsky laughed… "Do you mean, get past it…? Get a life, as they say…?"

"Well, something like that," said Mortie…. "But it seems like more than that. Like there actually was something… that made it so important…. At least to some people…. I know all of the basic stuff. You know Woodstock. Heck, some great bands…. My god, Led Zeppelin…, President Kennedy. We studied Martin Luther King. But is that it?"

His mother was hugely amused. "Why do you want to know?" she asked.

"I don't know…," he said. "Just something that's going on."

"Mortie…," said his mother.

"What?"

"Mortie… Do you remember that box of pictures in the attic I found you playing in that one time…"

"Oh sure, I used to go up there and dig around in that stuff…. The dresses and all of those antique pipes and things. Theatre props … I loved that attic. I used to go up there all the time when I was little, looking through those albums. Those were your friends from your theatre days…. What happened to all that stuff?"

"Mortie, that was me…"

He laughed. "No, I mean…" began Mortie. I'm serious."

"So am I," said his mother as they were pulling up to the Chrysopolis.

"And do you remember the dark haired guy with the long hair…?"

"Father…?! No…!"

"Oh no…! What a thought! No…!" She shook with laughter so that her dress glittered in the light through the window. "Oh, you are so funny… Bertram, a hippy? He was a fine man, but a hippie?! No, that was a…, a friend…."

"I still don't understand."

"Listen, Mortimer. Once, just for a while, a few people had a very good idea…. It really wasn't our idea. At the time, I thought it was…, but this idea had been coming for a long time. But, for a very brief while, we lived it. It was a good, and really a brave thing to do."

"What was it?"

"It was something simple. Not complicated. Anyone can do it. Even now when things are getting so confused. It was that people could live in their own way. Simply."

"Mother," laughed Mortie. "You live in a mansion; on two hundred acres…."

"True… And I love it," she said. "And I love my… things…. But that doesn't mean that the idea was bad. The idea was that they did not have to live the way others – that is, mostly their parents – had lived. That they could entertain themselves with whatever they wanted, so long as it did not hurt others or themselves.

"So…?" said Mortie. "Lots of people do that."

"A lot of people think they do. But mostly they're living for someone else. Mostly for their banks and credit card companies."

"True.... So what happened?"

She shrugged. "We were young. That was part of it. We smoked a little; actually a lot. And we had a lot of fun, too. But the main thing was that people heard. Some people from the big magazines heard and wrote about it."

"And...?"

"So, the people started coming. More and more came.... And the people that came weren't all nice. They didn't have good hearts. That's the way it always is when you're having a good time.... It's not the type of thing that works out if you try."

"And then...?"

"Oh... I don't know," she said airily. Nothing much. "We went our separate ways. We made our accommodations. Life happened, I guess. Look, Mortimer, old times are just old. They weren't that much. Now is more important."

"So don't try...?" said Mortie. "That doesn't sound like you..."

"No! No!" she exclaimed. "It's hard to explain." They were at the restaurant.

"It sounds like a lot of them didn't enjoy much ... After."

Rain began to streak the windows. "More or less," she said. "A lot of old hippies get bitter. It's like their lives stopped and they're confused. They're spoiled like little kids. They think they were owed a nice, happy life. Not the real ones…."

"The real ones…?"

"There were always fewer real hippies than everyone thought. Most were just play acting. I'm sorry…. I don't think much about those times any more…." They were in the porte-cochère of the Chrisopolis. A doorman opened the door. Mrs. Jablonsky got out. The rain dripped from the edge of the awning. She turned to him.

"Mortimer… How many really great parties have you been to in your life?"

"Parties?" he asked. "Of any sort?"

"Yes…."

He shrugged. "I don't know… Boy… Maybe a couple that I can remember…."

"That's right," she said. "That's my point. You never know when you're going to have a really good party, and you never know when you're going to find love. They don't happen all that often, so when you find it, hang on to it."

Seven

The Chrysopolis was a staid old country club located in an even staider and older stand of oaks at the northwest corner of the city. The wood floors creaked about as much as the bones of the members; or more accurately, as the wallets did as they opened. Club members were people who did not easily part with their dough.

Mortie retrieved his car and drove on over. He had not seen Gloria for years, and in truth, he hadn't seen much of her after the accident, what with being conked on the head and her being dressed in some sort of green paramedic togs. But, although that gave him a certain uneasiness, his real concern was running the gauntlet of his mother's friends, every one of whom could be counted upon to corner him on one pretense or another.

"Well, Mortimer, how are you?" said a very large woman in a voice somewhat like an out of tune cello.

"Hello, Mrs. Welchly," said Mortie. "I'm fine… And you?"

"How could I be? You never come to see me…" said Mrs. Welchly, in an injured voice. She seemed to be talking to him, covering him in her gaze, but the lamplight of her view was uninterrupted and included all of the incoming people. She moved slightly to improve her strategic view. Satisfied with things, she planted herself, adjusted her expansive bosom, and fixed her Cheshire cat smile upon her countenance like a bend in rock strata.

Mrs. Welchly… by her own judgment, the grandest of the granddames of the city, was also the Chairperson of the annual Police and Fireman Ball, the biggest charity event in the city. As far as anyone knew, she had been the chairperson since just after the last ice age, at any rate, for as long as anyone cared to remember. Mrs. Welchly did not wield any formal power, but a frown from her brought a certain terror among those who thought to get ahead in the bureaucracy of the city… for she *did* have power. She, or one of her many minions, were on every committee of any note in the city. They were those imposing rocks of society who, had anyone the courage to ask, would have ardently denied that they read anything but gardening magazines (perish the thought of reading a newspaper), but somehow missed nothing in the way of goings on in city society.

She was their undisputed leader. Unofficial, yes, but she ruled her flock with an iron hand. Her goal was influence. If one were in city government, she and her associates could usually do little in the way of advancement. But… make a serious stumble, and the whispering became intense. Mrs. Welchly took this position seriously. She felt it a civic duty to be aware of everything that was going on.

The phone rang all day.

"Elizabeth, dear…! I'm so glad you called!" A long pause while she settled back into a sunny chair and took a delicate sip of tea. "You don't say…," she would exclaim in her low, syrupy voice. "You *don't* say… Well, *I*, for one, am shocked…." Her voice would grow quiet and generously sad. "He isn't really our sort, is he, dear?" she would add, clucking her tongue. "Elizabeth, my dear, you and I see things the same way, don't we…? I know… I know. We should do *something*. Well, well, but for now, we will just have to wait. We will wait a bit… I will check with the others. Then… Well, we shall see… We shall *see* then, won't we…?"

The peak, the Mt. Everest of the year's social event, was the Police and Firemen's Ball. The P and F Ball, as it was called, was the largest charity event of the season. Attendance was noted, if not formally, by the matrons. As for the Police and Firemen's Charity Ball, anyone in city government would miss it at their peril.

The only fly in this ointment was that she was not Mrs. Constance Jablonsky.

Mrs. Welchly was well off, but she was not rich. She had minions, and thus, power of a sort… but she did not run in the same circles as Mrs. Jablonsky. Wielding the most sensitive personal political radar, she was aware of the extent of Mrs. Jablonsky's subtle maneuverings, for she too felt the effect of these activities, as one might, looking up at some distant overhead weather. But the most aggravating fact was that, despite all of her efforts – years of concentrated straining on Mrs. Welchly's part – Constance Jablonsky did not include her in her circle of friends. Although Mrs. Jablonsky was perfectly polite on those infrequent occasions that they met, for it was impossible that they would not meet occasionally, she did not go out of her way to greet Mrs. Welchly. Actually, she did not acknowledge Mrs. Welchly's existence at all.

Mrs. Welchly did not like that… Not one bit.

To someone as stubborn and single-minded as Mrs. Welchly, that indifference was an insult, an insult which had been repeated many times. And so, over the years, her attitude had slowly changed.

To intense hatred.

Yes, that's right, to a burning, smoldering, eye glittering hatred.

Not that she ever let anyone see this. All people are two people. There is the face they show the public, even their friends and their family. And then there is the face of the person that lives inside them. She had never told anyone this, for she was content to let everyone think she had always been a rock, a pillar of society that had stood in the middle of things. But at the core of her being she remembered. Oh yes, she remembered all too often and well; that childhood on the hardscrabble farm, her father, sunburned, unbending and harsh. Her mother, tired, worn by work. And above all, she remembered, from the earliest times, the burning desire to raise herself up in the world.

She had done it, too.

Step by step, she had climbed to a recognized place in this society. True, there had been that young man, a bright young man. He had loved her, too. But he wasn't like her. He seemed satisfied with less. Sometimes she thought of him. The others knew her place without her saying it. Though they did not know her background, they sensed that iron determination so that they, more often than not, bowed before the force of her will.

But Mrs. Jablonsky didn't.

In her, Mrs. Welchly saw someone who not only didn't bow, but who walked right by without so much as acknowledging her.

Oh no, open hatred would be an admission of defeat, and that was not going to happen. Her hatred of Mrs. Jablonsky was like a peat fire deep in the earth that cannot be seen on the surface, yet was smoldering under that generous smile.

"You remember my nephew Caswell, don't you?" asked Mrs. Welchly, smiling broadly, for she had heard that Mortie and Caswell Crogsly had been bosom enemies since childhood. This was a fortunate meeting. A fortunate meeting, and she was well seasoned to test these waters. She wanted proof.

"Certainly, I do," said Mortie, politely enough.

But Mrs. Welchly had just gotten started. "Oh *yes*," she said with a practiced chuckle. "I was just telling Caswell, here…" She ruffled a vast mass of drapery toward a tall, ruggedly handsome young man who didn't seem all that enthusiastic about talking, except that Mrs. Welchly held his arm in an unbreakable grip.

"Wasn't I, Caswell?" she continued. "I was just telling you that I hadn't seen that Mortimer at our little soirees in… how do they say it? … Heuh, heuh, heuh… a *coon's* age." She poked Crogsly. "He's terrifying criminals, I hear…. Heuh, heuh… Exciting, eh?"

"Hello, Jablonsky," said Caswell, a faint smile playing at the corner of his mouth. "I hear you're a policeman. I guess being a public *servant* keeps you busy…."

"Hello, Crogsly," replied Mortie. "I see you haven't managed to acquire lips yet."

"Eh…?"

Mrs. Welchly's eyes took on a certain glow. "Now, now, boys," she said, considering how to blow on these metaphorical embers to make a little fire. But to her palpable disappointment, Mortie appeared uninterested and drifted away. Not only that, but through main effort, Crogsly pried his arm from her grip, made his excuses, and drifted away also.

Mrs. Welchly let him go. She had heard enough. She hummed a little as she turned her attention to the scattering of people filtering through the door. She had learned what she wanted to know, and had confirmed something her intelligence network had inkled her about. She was happy, but not a sentimental person. She had learned something interesting. To most persons in her circle, little contretemps were interesting, but *merely* interesting. Mere gossip. But to her, they were not merely interesting. They were useful, and in this case, she had to think about it, to hoard it for future use. Useful, that is, if you knew how to use them… and she had spent years developing her techniques. The secret was judgment. It was her strength … and her solace. It was *nothing* to simply know things. Oh, certainly judgment was supreme. In order of make any use of it you had to taste the stew, and judge the strength of the bitter stew. This was a good one… This one had potential, and she carefully filed it in her personal mental filing cabinet. She thought of Mrs. Jablonsky. The heat in her chest grew.

How smug that woman was.

How smug to think that her one son, that poltroon, that marshmallow, would actually become something. Not if she could help it. She didn't know how this thing would be used. She did not know, but it had potential. She would see. She would see.

Her smile had never left her face. "Why Mrs. Swanson…!" she exclaimed. How nice to see you…"

"I say there, Mortie," said a tall, thin, mustache'd man in a dark blue sport coat with a *Yacht Club* decal on his lapel.

"Oh…, hi there, Mr. Blueheart… uh, *Captain* Blueheart," said Mortie. Captain Blueheart, in addition to being obsessively, insanely devoted to sailing, had apparently mastered the art of speaking without moving a muscle of his face. Exactly where the sound came from was unclear, perhaps it was his nose. One looked for any emotion in his face solely by the millimeter of the raising or lowering of his eyebrows, which expressed the whole gamut of emotion, actually eyebrow, since it was usually the right one that moved…, if any.

Captain Blueheart peered at Mortie through eye glasses so thick his eyes seemed to slosh around behind them like eggs rolling around in a bowl. "We haven't seen you at the slips this year have we… Eh Mortimer… At the *tiller*?"

"I'll get there soon, Captain Blueheart," said Mortie who liked sailing. "I've been a little busy."

"…eh…? What….? Ah yes, we heard something…. We're not all the main thing these days, but we *do* hear things, Mortimer…. Something about the *police,* I believe. Eh… Chasing the riff-raff… That sort of thing?

"Yes," said Mortie. "I'm a detective…."

"Ah…!" said Captain Blueheart, who nodded very slightly, or perhaps he may have swayed in some breeze; in any case, without the faintest expression on his face, save the slight twitching of an eyebrow. He then stared vaguely off at something.

"I was once in the police..." he said. An eyebrow moved slightly…

"Really?" said Mortie, who *was* surprised.

Captain Blueheart came to parade rest. He tilted his head slightly to the east and nodded. "WWII … Posted to the 3rd Army… Military Police…. Then OAS…. Tripoli 44'. A very droll affair.

Mortie was impressed. "How did you get there?"

"Oh, it was nothing," said Captain Blueheart waving off the question. "I had worked in the area... Istanbul and Tripoli and in Egypt..., couple of other postings. Clerked for my father's company, you know. Trading.... This and that... bric-a-brac, perfumes, oils, wholesale cloth... Perfumes were good. Profitable too... People didn't bathe as much then. Needed it. Nothing too much. Off and on for a couple of years. Knew a smattering of the Arabic... Attached to the British Legation.... Very droll. Touch and go there for a while."

"Dangerous...?"

"Dangerous...," repeated Captain Blueheart, fixing an owlish gaze on Mortie. "I should say so... Terrible. The dust... All that spicy food. Dealing with the British. That was enough to kill anyone.... Worked hell with one's digestion. Lucky to be alive..."

"That sounds bad," said Mortie. "How did you make it?"

"I'll tell you how," said Blueheart taking Mortie by the arm and pulling him close. He waved at some invisible horizon. "I knew how to *blend*.... Stayed out of the line of fire. A lot of men don't know how to do it... To *blend,* see..." He poked Mortie. "Blend eh...? That's the trick... But Mortie..., enough of that nonsense...." He clutched at Mortie's arm with an amazingly strong grip. "When are we going to see you at the *helm*....? The *helm,* Mortimer?"

"Well sir," said Mortie. "I've had to work quite a bit. We've been a little shorthanded."

“Nonsense…!” said Captain Blueheart. “Grab that tiller and don’t let go. All the rest is nonsense.”

There was a commotion. In the entryway, a knot of people surrounded someone. Captain Blueheart peered over there. “What the devil…? Don’t remember her…”

“It’s Gloria Aschenhult, I think,” said Mortie.

An eyebrow elevated. “Aschenhult, eh…? Went off to Europe, I heard. Thank god, she didn’t marry one of those Frenchmen. “My god! What lines! A gorgeous bit of trim, eh, Mortimer?”

Gloria came in greeting everyone, hugging this person and then that one. She was stunningly beautiful.

“Captain Blueheart! Is that you,” she said enthusiastically, hugging him and ignoring Mortie completely. She spent a few minutes describing a sailing trip in the Mediterranean. Captain Blueheart flushed, an event unheard of, at least in recent memory.

“Astounding girl eh? Sailing large, eh Mortimer?” said Captain Blueheart, watching Gloria head off toward some other friends. “My god, what lines! If I was your age… Haul anchor and set a course for that. That Crogsly fellow is tacking you. Cutting your wind, Mortimer…. Stealing your wind…!”

Gloria had seen Crogsly. She hugged him and they spent a long time talking animatedly together.

Mortie drifted around lamely for a while talking to this and that person. His uncle nodded, but that was about it. The

Mayor nodded and said hello. Mortie finally ended up leaning at the bar. He ordered a whisky, took a sniff, and felt a little sick. He sipped ice water.

He was seated at dinner with his friend Birdy Loosewright. Yes it was the Birdy who Gloria Aschenhult once tied to a tree and then forgot for a few hours. That, of course, was when they were teenagers. Birdy was now a corporate lawyer, a quirky, soft faced, young trial lawyer who looked as if, at any minute, he might turn into a middle aged successful lawyer. Birdy's expression, normally upbeat, was quite somber.

"What's with you…?" said Mortie. "A merger came unmerged; costing millions?"

"No… That I might be able to fix," said Birdy morosely, raising a forkful of Greek Salad to his mouth. "That's only money."

"So?"

"I'm on the Committee."

"What committee?"

"The P and F Ball," said Birdy.

Mortie was shocked. Birdy was too clever to be maneuvered onto a committee, at least one he wanted to avoid. "How?"

"Welchly got Mrs. Swenson to call my mother…"

"Oh my god…," said Mortie.

The music started. They watched as Gloria headed for the dance floor with Crogsly.

“I hear they dated when she was in Europe…,” said Birdy.

A cold feeling seeped into Mortie’s stomach. He started to say something, but stopped.

“Birdy…!” Gloria exclaimed, when the dance was over, hugging him. Birdy and a group gathered around Gloria. Mortie started over to join them.

His phone buzzed.

It was Blackie. “You busy?”

“Uh… No…. What’s up…?”

“There’s talk of a shipment coming.”

“What is it?”

“Don’t know… Hard stuff, I’ve heard… They wouldn’t talk that way about weed.”

“Any idea when?”

“Soon… That’s all…”

Alice Birdwright tucked herself into an indentation on the veranda smoking a cigarette and watching the crowd through open French doors. She took a drag on her cigarette and considered the crowd. She had been trying to identify the feeling within herself. Actually she had been trying to avoid it. She knew what it was. Thirty eight years old….

Bored.

This gig was too easy. Shepherding a retiree. Great. Lately she’d wondered if it was worth it. It barely strained her talents. She took a drag and crushed out the cigarette. She watched the crowd. Click, click, click, the faces registered, the backgrounds spun out: he runs a furniture factory, she a computer matching service, suspected of more than matching, there's Smith the real estate mogul, silver hair…, a very ruddy, unhealthy, overheated face, actually a very small mogul on a downhill run; on and on the faces flowed.

A group came in making a stir in the crowd. The Mayor and others greeted him enthusiastically, all the while trying to appear they weren't cloying. In the middle of that little crowd was a stocky man. The man did not smile much and did not seem to move much, as if he were anchored to a spot. The Mayor and some others drifted toward him. People swirled around him as if he were a planet and they were swirled into his gravity field. She had seen him before, a few times…. Meacham, yes Meacham, the governor's man, here for this type of gathering…. Not bad looking. Bear-like. Ought to lose the beard, though. He nodded gravely at a woman who practically threw herself into his arms. A tingle in her stomach when she watched him… Nice looking guy…

A breeze ruffled the drapes. She wrapped her arms around herself, and sucked on the cigarette, now interested in this, a component of her life, this categorization of the swirling unwashed. There was Mortie looking big and lame and uncomfortable, looking across at that gorgeous girl… what was her name? Oh yes, Gloria. Drop dead gorgeous. Poor guy, uncomfortable in this crowd. Looks like a big cream puff. Looks are deceiving though. He's got potential. He's stronger mentally than people think; vulnerable.

She'd stayed because of her mother. Oh she'd had plenty of offers to go back east, or even up to the state house in this or that capacity. She knew she was hot and smart and could do it anywhere. But she'd stayed. She couldn't go. Eight years of taking care of her and paying the hospital.

Music now… and the crowd raised the pitch of its sound. Someone laughed…, a high, hard laugh.

She lit another. It was over with her mother. And even that felt a loss. Odd wasn't it, how that everyday routine, that very hard routine, get up every day, go to the nursing home… or the hospital at the end… even that routine became part of one's life, and the loss of it made an empty space.

Now there was nothing to stop her from using her talent to get somebody up there. Up there as high as the talent would take them. She needed it. A project. She watched Mortie. How much fire is in that belly? Don't know. She watched him. Chief Powell nodding to Mortie… trying too hard to talk to the Governor's man. There was her boss, at the end of his career.

A dead end.

She lit another and her eyes roamed… and stopped. That's interesting. Why was Mrs. Welchly, with a frozen smile on her face, staring daggers at someone? Who was it? She followed the direction of the look. Why, the woman was glaring at Mortie! Why?… What possibly could that be about? And then, as if Mrs. Welchly had a radar that detected people's gaze, she turned, searching the room. Alice edged toward a shadow and watched. But just as quickly as it showed, that hatred faded from Mrs. Welchly's face, replaced by a benign benevolence toward all.

A voice.

"Alice…?" the mayor was calling her… "Hiding out here, are you? Come on. We need an independent opinion…."

She ground out her cigarette. "On what…?"

The mayor laughed. "The Governor's chances…."

"Squat-ola…," said Alice and dove back into the gathering. The mayor was smiling at her. They were all smiling at her the way people smile at people who wield power, the look she had known since she had been a New York ward baby. She glowed. She loved it. "Do you know Jim Meachem?" the Mayor said.

She extended her hand and smiled. Nice brown eyes… "No…, but I've heard about you…," she said.

"Anything good?" said Meachem smiling back

"You know how it is," she said, flashing a wide smile. "Politics. Further evidence required…," she said.

Eight

"Do you get the feeling that we're nowhere in this thing?" said Mortie.

They were sitting in Blackie's absolutely nondescript Chevy sedan parked at the back row of a shopping center parking lot with a hundred or more cars whose occupants felt that eleven thirty at night was the best time to shop.

"Well, we're further along than we were.... What do you mean, we're nowhere...? There's a lot of talk. Everyone on the street is talking about it...." He twiddled with some knobs on the radio. A foreign voice suddenly began shouting unintelligibly from the radio. It went on and on....

"What is that?" frowned Mortie at the noise coming out of the radio.

"Tehran, I think," said Blackie turning it down. "I get them at night when I want to stay awake. Blackie twiddled with some knobs and then shut it down. "It's all perfectly legal.... You'd be surprised how public things are on the airwaves. Oh... Doc Weisman called. Senevitch didn't die from the bullet. He drowned. And he had drugs in him. And his hands show signs of a struggle."

They watched in silence as a woman and a man loaded about a dozen cases of Cola into the back of an SUV.

"Do we know where…?"

"No…."

"We don't know who is involved. A guy drowns…. After some sort of struggle…." said Mortie. "Then he's dragged to a tree, tied, and used for target practice?"

"Uh huh…."

"Why?"

Blackie shrugged. "I don't know… To scare someone…?

"And there's some sort of new shipment coming and some very good dope."

"Right…" said Blackie.

"Maybe there's nothing… No connection."

"I've thought of that… But people don't do that for no reason…."

"No, I don't suppose," said Mortie. "They definitely had something in mind. We have to figure it out. And we've got to figure it out… Fast. I have the feeling that if we don't get it right, it will be a while before anyone does. Let's get the phone information for every single person in the park or connected to the park. Can we get DNA data?"

"Without a search warrant?" asked Blackie.

"No… The court wouldn't give us that broad a search. Even a loosey-goosey judge. So until we get one, we get what we can. Can we get someone on-site to collect?"

"Like what…?"

"Cigarette butts. Soda cans. Multiples, if you can."

"On everyone?"

"Everyone.... Somebody's got their fingers in this."

"We can try," said Blackie. "I'll get help from IT. We can do a lot. I can build a phone contact profile of everyone. Oh, by the way... Speaking of tech support, you got lucky on the match books you picked up."

"Yes?"

"He wrote phone numbers on them. Probably a habit of his. He'd throw them in the drawer. Probably forgot about them or thought it a clever way to hide something in plain sight. You just write on the inside, close it up and leave it laying in a drawer. There were quite a few of them. Some had names."

"The Purloined Letter..."

"What...."

"A Poe story about a criminal who hid something in plain sight," said Mortie. "No one is going to look there. Besides, they wouldn't see anything if they did. Who is the hit on the print...?"

"Guy, name of Jackson. He is the guy who did sixty days in the Brownsville Jail on that dope beef."

"And?"

"Nothing. No further record. But...."

"What...?"

"We got lucky on one thing. The phone numbers on match books? One was crossed off like you'd really want it to be crossed off. Inked. Magic marker... Not readable."

“And…?”

“Tech was able to send it off to a lab. Some spectrometer thing. Sorts out discrete ink types. Number popped out like script.” He handed Mortie a short printout. “Here is that number and some of the others… We’re going to check that one against all current databases. We’re in the process of doing a macro profile of all communication for Parks. If we had a warrant, we could do more….”

Mortie was fixing the numbers on the list in his head. “Good… We need to get a little more information to obtain a warrant. We have to keep making progress. Do it legally, but don’t tell anyone….”

“There’s one more thing I’ve heard,” said Blackie.

“What’s that..?”

“There’s a very bad person behind all of this.”

“Oh…?”

Blackie shook his head. “Mortie… These people are scared shitless of this guy. Really scared. I mean, the way they look when they talk about…”

“Who is it?”

“That’s it…” said Blackie. “No one seems to know who he is, or what he looks like. They’re scared to talk. If he says someone works, they work. If he says they die, they die. People are terrified to cross him. A very mean guy…”

“Or woman,” said Mortie.

“Or woman,” repeated Blackie.

An insistent beam of blinding sun shone mercilessly through the blinds the next morning. The phone was jangling.

"Mortie," said a cheery voice, somewhat like a musical table saw with a New York accent. "Are you up…?" It was Alice Birdwright, she, of the electric red hair and habitual wide-eyed innocent look.

Mortie sat bolt upright. "Yes, of course," he lied, a picture of Alice exploding into his mind. He staggered to his small kitchen.

"I heard about the accident, Mortie…," Alice said soothingly. "Are you feeling okay?"

"I feel fine…."

"Alice could come over and make you breakfast. Are you still in bed…?"

"Alice…, said Mortie. "I know when you're joking…. Quit it…."

"Too bad," she said, her voice resuming its buzz saw rasp. "In that case, get your tail in here…. There's a small problem…."

"What is it??"

"Something about Ortwell Katzman…"

"Katzman?"

"And some sort of department matter. Just be here…."

"Okay… When?"

"Eleven…. Use the back door, please," said Alice. "People are just waiting to get a picture of you and the Chief together so they can plaster it all over the place."

They spent the early part of the morning systematically tracking down and interviewing all of the employees they could find who had been working in the park when the body was found. The day was sunny. Around ten, a breeze like a warm wet blanket began to sway the vast acreage of flowers in the park. Very quickly, the sun began to beat mercilessly down upon them.

"I don't know," said Ortiz the foremen, wiping sweat from his brow with his hat and looking off toward the river with exactly zero enthusiasm. "We get a lot of guys working here. It's hard work and we don't pay them that much." He stared off across the beautiful verdant swale. "They come and go. I suppose I could get you a list." In the end they found nothing.

They were walking an asphalt path to their cars. They rounded a large planting of Arborvitae and practically ran over a short, jaunty looking man who was sitting on a bench with his feet stuck out in their path. The man had a black cowboy hat on and boots. It was Ortwell Katzman.

"Howdy, boys," he said.

"Hello, Mr. Katzman," said Mortie. "How are you?"

Katzman tilted back his black cowboy hat. "Fine as a new ripe peach, sir," he said, smiling a tight little smile. "Yes sir, fine as a Georgia peach. It surely is good to see two of my men back in god's own garden." Mortie could see his own weirdly contorted reflection in Katzman's mirror sunglasses. Katzman retrieved a nail file and began touching up his nails.

"Where might y'all be going?" he smiled horribly. "That is..., if y'all would allow me the liberty to ask?"

Mortie pointed at the street. "We're about finished up here, Mr. Katzman. We're just leaving...."

"Leaving? ... Leaving? Just like that, y'all are leaving? An' just when we all was gettin' to appreeechate y'all's various qualities."

"We enjoyed our...," began Mortie.

"I do not think I like that...," said Katzman.

"Now look, Mr. Katzman," said Blackie. "We're really grateful that you let us work the park under cover. But ... well, what with the victim..."

"*Let* y'all work in the park?" shot back Katzman, who then stood up and stuck out his chest, his voice suddenly becoming the hard south. "I l*et* you all right... Do y'all think ah care about some dead guy? And do you think I care if you're cops? Well I am heah to disabuse you of that notion. I don't care. Let me infoam you boys of this leetle fakt. I didn't *let* you work in the park." He pointed a hard finger at them. "We made a deal. We made a deal, and where ah come from, a deal is a deal, body or no body. I didn't get my end of it, so we're going to pe-lay it out. I want you guys back on the job." He smiled slowly. "Pronto.... The Festival..., mah festival is drawin' close. And as far as I'm concerned, y'all are just labor. You ain't much, but every backbone counts."

"But Mr. Katzman," started Mortie.

Katzman held up a palm. "Don't start, Jablonsky. Don't even start. This is our busy time of the year. You aren't done with your end of it. Soooooo. I expect you two maalingerers to show up with the sun…." He pointed a finger at Mortie. "Or you can tell Powell that there'll be hell to pay."

"My god, can he do that?" said Blackie.

Mortie shrugged. "Ah do not… I say, ah, do not think, sir… that he can…"

"Mortie…!"

"Oh sorry…. All I can do is bring it up with Groatly and the Chief."

They were almost to their car when they saw three men ankling across a parking lot.

"There's some parks guys," said Blackie, pointing. One of the men had long stringy hair and elusive slate colored eyes. The other two were chatty and friendly. One of the two, a short waddle-y looking sort, shook out a cigarette and lit it.

"Nah… We never saw that guy," he said. "Lot of that in the park.

"We weren't around," said the other. "Heard he was shot…. Never met the dude…." He seemed to be looking past Mort and Blackie at an approaching man. A look of fear covered the man's face.

"What the heck's with you?" said Blackie looking around.

"It's the *man*…" said one of them almost inaudibly. He backed up and then disappeared in back of a large bush.

Blackie, alarmed, turned to look. "What…? The drug kingpin…?"

"Worse…!" said one of the two remaining.

"*Much* worse…," said the other

"What…?" said Mortie.

"It's the *Union* Guy…"

He was a man as mild and unhurried as a summer day; olive skinned, with slack, but neat, dark hair. He wore a silvery brown suit. The breeze ruffled his pant leg. Except for coal black eyes, he was the gentlest looking person Mortie had ever seen, although one might add in retrospect, one of those people who are hard to see clearly, as if they are continuously going in and out of focus.

"Thank god, I found you..." he said in a voice like molasses. "We heard this thing that has happened…."

"You heard this thing?" said Mortie. "What thing?"

The man handed them each a business card. "It's an outrage. I rushed right over."

"An outrage? Where?" said Mortie, raising up to his full impressive height. "Where…? We take care of outrages… Wait… I have no idea what you're talking about. Who are you?"

"I am Feldman…." He fumbled in a leather portfolio. "I am your union representative," said the man.

They looked at him blankly. "We're in a union?" said Blackie.

"What did you say the outrage was?" added Mortie.

"Why… your being assigned to work in Parks…" said Feldman. Reddish pinpoints of light glowed and faded in the coal black centers of his eyes. "We shall not stand for this."

Mortie felt relieved. He waved at Feldman. "Oh… Oh, look see, it's okay. We aren't actually parks workers. We've got another assignment. It's a police matter, really. So you can…"

Feldman put his hand on Mortie's shoulder comfortingly. "You brave, brave man," he said. He seemed as if he might cry…. "If the public only knew…."

"Are you sure you've got the right people?" said Mortie. "We're cops, not some victims. We help people…" He gestured toward Blackie. "This is Lt. Blackman and I'm…

"Lieutenant Jablonsky…" interrupted Feldman dabbing at an eye. I know…."

"What union would that be?" said Mortie.

"Why the Associated City and Hotel Workers Union United…."

"ACHUU?" repeated Mortie. He winked at Blackie. "Okay, Mr. whatever-your real name is, I don't know who put you up to this, but the joke's over. I suppose it's those guys in the Ready Room. We've got a lot to do, so if you don't mind…"

"Oh no!" exclaimed Feldman, leaning close. "Oh no, no, we're *deadly* serious…. I want to help you…. Actually I *have to* help you. I'm your representative. It's my job…."

"So ACHUU is our union …?"

“Yes…” said Feldman eagerly…” Yes, yes! Isn’t it wonderful? Our motto is *We’re nothing to sneeze at.* Isn’t that great? We’ve organized the whole state.”

“We’re in with the hotel workers?” said Mortie, who was beginning to believe Feldman was actually serious. “We’re cops and we got put in with hotel workers?”

“Well, of course…,” said Feldman. “You’re all public servants, aren’t you?”

“I suppose so…” said Mortie. “I hadn’t really thought about it too much…. But… Wait! This is all ridiculous…. We appreciate you looking us up, but we don’t need any help, Mr. Feldman. We can handle our own problems, if any come up….”

“Oh, but that’s where you’re wrong,” said Feldman waving a finger in negation. “You perhaps misheard my previous comment… I *have* to help you. I *must*... It’s my job description. I’d get fired if I didn’t…. You wouldn’t want that, would you…?”

Mortie looked at Blackie….

Feldman seemed intensely disappointed at their response. “And… most importantly,” he added, recovering his composure. “It’s in the contract.”

“Contract?” they said in unison.

Exactly…,” said Feldman, happily now. “It’s spelled out precisely in the collective bargaining agreement of August 1, 2005, since updated…. I have a copy back at the office. I’d have brought it to show you, but it weighs a little too much to lug around.

“It weighs too much to carry?”

“Well, it is a little awkward,” said Feldman. “But it does serve. It does serve, sir,” said Feldman with an intense chuckle, a sound that caused them both to shiver. “That’s our little joke, of course. Only Congress weighs their contracts.”

“Congress…! You deal with Congress…?”

A cold light of amusement, like a morning sun without heat, grew in Feldman’s eyes. “Some of our best customers,” he said gravely. “Congress loves the law.”

“Well, of course,” said Blackie.

“Particularly when they don’t have to follow them. All bills are now weighed. They haul them around in wheel-barrows. They operate upon one well established principal.”

“I can’t believe I’m asking this,” said Mortie. “But what principal is that?”

“That the less you have to say, the more words you should take to say it,” said Feldman. “Though I might add…” he added, raising a finger to make a point… “that one certainly wouldn’t want to be in a union with a contract of less than three pounds. I *know* I wouldn’t.”

“I should not think so…,” said Mortie. “How much, if I might ask, is ours?”

“Perfect. Not too light. You wouldn’t want to be light. No one would take you seriously. Right at the industry average. Just the right amount… Obviously something that took a while to get negotiated. But not too weighty, so you can’t be accused of furrowing.”

"Furrowing…?" said Blackie.

"Dragging our feet and standing in the way of progress."

"So you're our representative whether we want it or not?" said Blackie impatiently.

"Yes, of course," said Feldman, flipping through some papers. "You are P-10s, aren't you?"

"'P-what's…?" said Mortie.

"Uhhh, Mortie," said Blackie. "I think he's right. I remember something about that in the book we were supposed to read during our orientation."

"That thing was longer than War and Peace!" Mortie exclaimed. It was…"

"Exactly," interrupted Feldman…. "But..," he said, raising a finger to make a point. "If you *had* read it, Section 10, subsection 3-B lists the general parameters of your respective classifications. Which… you were provided in the addendum supplied upon your assignment. You did review *that,* didn't you?"

"Of course…," they said in unison.

"Then you should be aware that you have been assigned out of your contractual slot."

"Now, wait," said Mortie irritably. "The boss assigns us and we go. It's not up to us…."

"Oh, but that's where you're wrong!" said Feldman. "Subsection B of section 4 states clearly that *any reassignment of the contractual integer…*" He pointed at them. "That's you… The CI. *Any* reassignment of the CI automatically shall generate a review by said Union

Representative; the UR." He pointed at himself. "That's me. I'm the UR."

"Is that all?" said Mortie. "Just that we're… reassigned?"

"Oh no!" cried Feldman. "That's just a start. In the case of the CI being reassigned TDY, that is, Temporary Duty, in another working environment, said alternative working conditions for the CE shall include all of those conditions obligated to the CI." He pointed at them. "That's you: Unsanitary working conditions. Breaks that do not meet contractually applied standard for length. No lower back support. That right there alone is enough for me to get a hundred protesters here. No visible porta-potties."

"Porta-potties?"

"Of course," said Feldman. "Personal Sanitary Units… PSU's…. Section 8, Subsection 12, Item B says, if I may take the liberty of recalling it exactly, 'One portable Personal Sanitary Unit, as defined in the national standard, shall…' please note it says 'shall' as opposed to 'may'… '*shall b*e provided in such a manner such that no worker has to walk more than three hundred feet.' That's up, by the way… We went for two hundred feet, but…" He seemed sad at this. "We had to settle for three hundred feet. No worker shall have to walk more than three hundred feet to utilize a visible sanitary facility."

"Or run if we keep eating breakfast at that greasy spoon over on 6th," laughed Blackie.

Feldman's black eyes narrowed. It certainly must have been a coincidence, but it seemed to Mortie that the sky darkened slightly. "These matters are not in the least bit funny, Lt. Blackman."

"What else?" said Mortie.

"Inappropriate uniforms subjecting the worker to ridicule – That alone is grounds for leave of absence and medical treatment; possible contravention of the American Disability Act; non-standard, foreign-produced, working equipment – an obvious contravention of the Buy American provision…"

"We've got to go," said Blackie.

"Remember," said Feldman. We're here for you! And we're nothing to sneeze at. What do you want done? I can have three hundred picketers here in two hours."

"We'll think about it," said Mortie. "See you later, Feldman."

"I don't think I'd want to get on that man's bad side," said Blackie.

"No," said Mortie. "That might be a mistake."

Nine

"Well… Yes…" Chief Powell coughed as he and Mortie made their way down a long, empty hallway. "I suppose technically I may have agreed you would spend several weeks with Katzman…. Technically. But look, we've got to focus on the problems at hand."

"He says three weeks…."

Powell nodded and laughed again. "So what's a week or two…? It's really not that serious. It's sort of a joke."

"He doesn't seem to think so…," said Mortie. "Plus… he mentioned an option of some sort."

"It was a *joke*," laughed Powel, waving the mere idea away. "We all have to have a little humor in our lives."

"I dunno," said Mortie. "Katzman seemed perfectly serious to me. He seemed really *mad* that we left. He's mad at you…."

Chief Powell stopped and then proceeded on. "At me…? Why me, for god's sake? I guess, yes, there might have been some talk of an option period." He chuckled. "You might have to play along…."

"An option?" repeated Mortie. "You optioned us? Like baseball players?"

The Chief shrugged. "Well… Not really like baseball players."

"What's the difference?"

"Well, for one thing," said the Chief, stopping and pantomiming a throwing motion, "you can't turn the double play."

"Feldman thinks it's the sort of thing we ought not to be doing."

The Chief stopped. "Feldman?"

Mortie nodded. "Yes… The union guy."

A cloud passed over the Chief's face. "You've met him?"

"Just…. ACHUU…"

"Gesundheit…"

"Says our contract doesn't allow for that."

"We all have to do things we don't want to," said the Chief. He resumed his walk.

"He says *you* don't," said Mortie. "Says you're management. He said something about a demonstration. Work stoppage and that sort of thing."

Chief Powell stared at Mortie. "Are you threatening me?"

"Oh, good god, no!" exclaimed Mortie. "Never. It's just that he… Feldman, that is…"

The Chief was still staring at him. He took a deep breath and then exhaled. "I'll see what I can do," he said.

They went into the conference room. Mortie was startled to see a bored looking Lt. Iverson slouched in a chair at their meeting.

"Chief," started Captain Groatly. "I hope you knows we're supporting Mortie here an' Blackie wit' everyt'ing we got." .

"A couple of Boy Scouts playing cops," muttered Lt. Iverson. He polished his sunglasses.

"What was that?" said an astonished Captain Groatly.

Mortie was silent.

"Yes… what would you suggest, Lt. Iverson…?" said Chief Powell.

Iverson shrugged. "I'm not in charge…."

Powell leaned forward. "So you object, but you don't have any suggestions?"

"Well, I don't know," said Iverson lazily. "But, I think it's a waste of time to be working the park victim when there's other priorities. That's all…"

"Mortie?" said Chief Powell.

"Here we go," muttered Iverson.

"We think there's a dope connection involved in this affair…," started Mortie.

"What evidence…?" interrupted Iverson.

"Wait!" said Captain Groatly. "You've had your chance. Let him finish…"

"As I said, we think there is a dope connection involved in this thing," said Mortie as calmly as he could. There has been a lot of talk on the street. As of this point, we can't prove it, and we need a little more...."

Iverson snorted.

Mortie was an extremely calm person, but at this outburst, he turned to Iverson.

"Why do you want us off this case, Lieutenant?"

Iverson flushed. "What are you implying...?"

"Not a thing...," said Mortie.

"How much time do youse boys need, Mortie?"

"Two weeks...?" said Mortie. "Really, we don't know. If we have to, we'll work off the books."

"Well, boise," said Groatly addressing Mort and Blackie, "we're unfortunately short-handed. We've got other priorities. Wrap up as fast as possible, but no shortcuts. You better wrap this ting up dis week if you don't get any more leads... Get a report to me and let's get on with our other cases."

"Yes, sir," Mortie said, glancing at Iverson.

"*No, sir...*" he thought.

"You know we can't do it in a week," Blackie said. Night... They were cruising again. Blackie was twiddling with his phone. "In the first place, we need to catch them in the act. And there's no guarantee that this next delivery will happen any time soon...."

"I know..."

"Well, what do we do?"

Mortie wheeled the sedan through two blocks of traffic. “I have one idea. It might actually help.... But it will mean more work.”

“What is it?”

“Well...,” said Mortie. “Suppose we let it be known that we’ve been taken off the park case and assigned to chop shop duty. We submit our report and then wait....”

Blackie nodded. “The perpetrators would hear about it and think the field was clear. Where do we start?”

“Well, we’ve got a week to make a big fuss; to bring the heat up on people.”

Ten

Early in its history, the city had been a major flour milling and lumbering center. Much bread was generated from this industry, plus many large, ugly mansions. Sadly, about all that was left of it were old, dusty pictures of Cotillions with stalwart-looking men with funny haircuts, and inanely grinning young women, who had nothing to worry about except the decision about what to wear for dinner.

The Mill District was an area of degraded concrete structures to the north of Riverside Park, between 3rd Street and River Road, looking in the morning mist like art; pale white spires, weather-beaten, and old. One concrete elevator, sticking up in the mist, had vacant, empty windows, and two huge, accusatory, ghostly eyes, the remains of an enormous faded face peering out from behind a giant bouquet of wheat sprigs. Here and there, pieces of these structures had fallen into the empty streets. But on the whole, the mill spires stood stubbornly upright, and though there were many of them, there was an aloneness, a loneliness to the Mill District. The spires were constructed of concrete and steel, built by men who thought things should last.

The Mill District had once generated the ingredients for bread. Now, it mainly generated lawsuits. One segment of the population saw them as an eyesore. Another group saw opportunity. But the Mill District had been prone to flooding.

"Trouble is, it don't flood enough to wash it away," said one councilman. "Too bad."

I mention all of this not because I'm interested in urban geography, but because the boys had been ricocheting around the city like pin balls, and it was that Mill District they were now driving by.

"What's with him…?" said Mortie, pointing toward a man who had seen them and was sidling toward a gap in the ruined buildings. He gestured toward the side of the street. "Pull over there…. Police…!" yelled Mortie at the man. "Wait…! We want to talk…."

The man ran.

"Drive around," said Mortie, pointing. But Blackie had already stopped and was out of the car running after the man. He disappeared through a concrete littered gap in a wall. Mortie slid over and jammed the car into gear, drove two blocks south, turned into a street, cursed when he saw the street blocked, backed out, spun the car around, and drove the car to a spot he hoped was the other side of the ruin. Gaunt and worn-looking ruins rose up on either side of him. Mortie entered through a gap in some rusted, broken fencing. He could hear the city noises in back of him, but nothing else. He waited. After a few minutes, he moved forward toward where he hoped Blackie would be. He moved slowly, watching for movement. He heard voices. He climbed into a vacant concrete structure.

It was Blackie, standing with his weapon out in the middle of a miniature field of tall, intensely green plants. Two young men, one a stocky Hispanic, the other a hulking creature with a faded John Deere baseball cap, were backed against a wall.

"Who are you?" asked Blackie, flashing his badge….

"Hey…. Like…, I'm Jesus," said the Mexican edging toward a gap in the wall that had once been a door. "We were just… wondering…."

"Stay where you are," ordered Blackie. "It's dope," he said to Mortie. "Marijuana." He was preparing to arrest the two men.

He ripped some leaves from a plant and held them up. "They're cultivating marijuana. Big plants, too…."

"No… Really? Is it Marijuana…?" said the squatty one, trying for an innocent expression. "We're like pacho, guys… We don't know how to farm." He pointed to the hulking oaf…. "Maybe Burt does…. He's like a hillbilly from someplace in the sticks. He's so stupid he has to be told when to wipe his butt…." He pointed toward the door. "We'll just be getting along."

"Whaaat…?" said Burt, scowling at his partner. He swept back a mop of stringy hair. "Stupid…? Who you calling a billy, you fat, dummy greaseball…" He grabbed

Jesus and tried to get him in a headlock, but Jesus really had no neck to speak of, so Burt slipped and fell onto the floor.

Jesus laughed and was going to pick him up, but Burt grabbed his leg, which caused Jesus to fall over also. They began rolling around on the floor punching ineffectually at each other.

Mortie and Blackie stood watching.

Some dust floated up.

"Boys…! Boys!" said Mortie quietly….

Jesus and Burt stopped fighting. They sat up.

"Is it medical marijuana…?" asked Mortie.

This question slowly sunk into Burt's head. "Medical…?"

"Yes…," said Mortie. "Someone must be growing this for their own medical use…."

"Hey… Yeah, man," said Jesus, being quicker on the uptake. He got up, lifting up Burt too. He dusted him off a little. "It's like medical…. It's for medical purposes only…. He flexed his shoulder. "It's the only thing that helps, man…. My eyes, too…."

"It's terrible…," said Burt solemnly … A life is a terrible thing to waste…."

"But you need a permit for that…."

"Oh….?"

"It's a crime if you haven't got the permits," said Mortie mildly. "A felony…. Ninety days, minimum, for this amount. Either of you guys been in…?"

They stared at him.... "No...! No...!" they said in unison. "We don't know nothing...."

"So, this stuff isn't yours?"

"Oh no...!"

"Look guys," said Mortie. "In that case, you've got about thirty seconds to disappear...."

"And leave these guys with the dope...?" said Blackie incredulously.

Jesus gazed at the marijuana wistfully. "Could we take a few plants? I'm learning how to make rope, and...."

"Beat it!" said Mortie. "If we see you again, here you'll be in lockup so fast you'll think you're on the trip of your life... Or worse. And don't come back. We'll send someone to get rid of this little farm.

The two men eased out the door. They ran.

"Shouldn't we call someone?" said Blackie.

But Mortie was already leaving. "Common.... Those two idiots aren't a danger to anyone but themselves. Call someone to get rid of this stuff. They won't be back today and this stuff will be gone before tonight. Let them go. It's a waste of county money to throw them in jail."

He pointed in the general direction of where he hoped the car was. "Let's go."

Blackie was quiet for a while. "Mortie..."

"Yes...?"

"The law is the law...."

"It is..." said Mortie nodding. "I know."

“So we should have run them in,” said Blackie. “Let the DA decide whether to prosecute….”

“In the first place,” said Mortie. “If we hauled in everyone we found who was standing next to some dope, we’d haul in half the country. It grows wild everywhere around here. Secondly, connecting those two idiots to it would be almost impossible.”

“But that stuff wasn’t wild,” said Blackie. He had a dissatisfied expression on his face.

“So you’d haul in every speeder?”

Blackie thought for a moment. “Yes…” he said. “Each and every one…. The law doesn’t say it is illegal to *sort of* go over a certain speed. “It says it is illegal and it’s our responsibility to enforce the law.” He laughed. “Those guys were something…”

“We’ll get the real guys…” said Mortie. “Find out if all of the flowers the park uses are planted full grown. And can you get find a history of electricity use at the park?”

“Electricity use? ….,” said Blackie. “I don’t know. Maybe… I can try.”

Mortie’s phone buzzed. “Hello, Mortie!”

“Francine…?”

“It be me, dear. The *kewlest* bean in the bean bag.”

“Look, I’m a trifle busy. Can I get back to you?”

“You still working park victim?”

“We’re going to be off that for a while now… I can’t really talk about it….”

“And assigned to what?”

“There’s been a lot of auto theft and we’ve…”

“Not the UOAI?”

“The what?”

Francine cackled. “The unrequited ownership auto industry.”

“Possibly…,” said Mortie.

“See, that bothers me.” Francine said. “Why would you get put on the auto theft gig? I’m no cop, dear, but I hear that’s a dead end show….”

“It’s a big problem…”

“No doubt, sweetie…. I’m sure the auto insurance industry is working day and night and weeping over it as we speak. Wasn’t Lt. Iverson and his partner Kline schlepping that gig…?”

He took a sip. “Umm… yes….”

“Otherwise known as Kline Motors, I might add.”

“What do you mean ‘Kline Motors’?”

“Oh nothing…. Just some tweetie talk….”

“What…?”

“Iverson’s partner Kline…”

“What about him…?”

“Ooo… You are a puppy, Mortie…. Nothing that I can put in my newspaper and not get sued… or worse. Kline has a rep as a very mean man, not averse to breaking a face to get what he wants. And to bend an elbow, by the way.”

“Where..?”

A pause… "Some cowboy place on south central. I hear it's a rough joint. People like me don't go there. Particularly since he knows me. And hates me enough to stuff me in a sack and throw me into the river…."

"What else…?"

"Nothing you can spread on bread and eat."

"What the heck does that mean?"

Silence. "Come on, Francine…"

"Mortie…, I'm not getting into that… But I'll say this: When you have a good deal going, why stop it?"

"I don't believe it," said Mortie.

"The path to glory is long, Mortie, and the gate is narrow. See you at the P and F Ball. Bye, bye Mortie."

Where are we going now?" asked Blackie as they hurried down the street.

"I'm not entirely sure…," said Mortie. "It was just a number on one of the matchbooks. On this one though there was a name. An author. He comes to this place every year. He's well known."

"An author? He knew an author?" said Blackie. "How could an author have anything to do with it?"

"I don't know, but it's on the way to where we're going. I think we should run it down.

Blackie was dubious. "I guess…."

"He comes to spend the summer. I think it's an artist's colony."

"An artist's colony?" repeated Blackie, looking at him sharply. He was always a little suspicious of Mortie's penchant for hanging around bookstores or literary inquiries. "That's why you want to do this, isn't it? I've never heard of an artist's colony here. We really don't have the time."

"Well, it's a big city…," said Mortie vaguely.

They turned off of Central Avenue to the west toward some sharp, cliff-like hill. The street climbed sharply. There was a section of the city where, though still developed with old brownstones, the land rose sharply into gloomy, forested ravines. The address they were heading for was sandwiched between two buildings; the first, a tiny brownstone with a very sharp, peaked roof, very much like a church. This church-like structure, covered with pleasant green ivy, was in front of a large, square, undistinguished building. On a sandstone frontispiece in faded sandstone, seemingly very old, were some curious inscribed markings.

"I am Beatrice," said a tiny woman with dark hollows under her eyes who met them on the porch of the building. "We don't get many police here…." She shifted uncomfortably, and darted a surprisingly hostile look up at the sun. She grimaced and turned back to them. "This sun… my skin."

"We were looking for a Mr. Preshion," said Blackie showing his badge.

Mortie stared at the inscriptions on the building, trying to remember his Latin.

"What does it say?" said Blackie.

"Can't make it out...," said Mortie, still trying to remember his Latin. It says. "*To... To Create Is...*"

"It says, "To Create is to Die," said Beatrice, from behind them. She waved abruptly. "Come in, if you're coming..."

Mortie was looking at several gargoyles leering down at them from under the overhang of the hip roof. "So this is an artist colony?"

"Yes, it is," she said, making a peculiar motion toward the hip of the roof or perhaps the inscription. "In summers, we have groups who come here to be with visiting authors." She motioned. "We can go in and see, but I'm not sure whether he is available. He works most mornings." She turned to them and stopped. "Please, when we go in, do not talk to the artists. They are working and don't like to be bothered."

"What is it, like a zoo?" joked Blackie.

Beatrice stopped and stared at him.

She led them in. Mortie seemed to remember that the building was on a low rise. But as soon as they had entered, it seemed to Mortie as though they were descending into it. Not only that, but they walked down and around several corners, so that Mortie seemed to lose his sense of direction. They continued descending. In a while, there was a vague light ahead and he realized that though the building was large and square, it had an interior courtyard around which the building was built, and that faint light filtered down from above.

The occupants worked on four or five different levels. They passed a number of halls filled with little cubicles within which men and woman seemed to be toiling intensely. A muttering came from one of the tiny cubicles. Within was a pale, little man who was staring at a pile of books. Strangely, the books seemed wet with printers' ink. It was hard to hear in passing, but the man seemed to be muttering over and over. "Sell… sell…" or something to that effect. It was hard to say. Whether he sensed their presence, Mortie didn't know, but he suddenly turned and looked at them beseechingly. Mortie wanted to stop and visit, but Beatrice gripped his arm with startling, claw-like strength, and whispered "suuuush," and so they left the man and kept on.

They passed more and more people and soon entered the courtyard. Here there were lots of people, most sitting on a terrazzo plaza on one end of the courtyard. They were sipping coffee and other drinks and talking animatedly.

It was uncomfortably hot and stuffy, but the writers seemed to be perfectly comfortable. Some were hunched over computers.

"Man, it's warm in here," said Blackie, tugging at his shirt which had begun to stick to his skin.

Beatrice, their guide, seemed perfectly comfortable.

"Aren't you hot?" he said to her.

She laughed. "Oh no…! I was born into it, I guess. Writers are mostly little hot house flowers. They love it. Just look at them…!"

“Preshion…?” said Mortie.

Beatrice peered around. “Not here, I think.”

Mortie looked, too. There were a goodly number of lights, but the courtyard was so large and the glass atrium ceiling so far above that it seemed to allow only a pale light and wistful glow on everything, particularly on the faces of the writers. In a minute or two, though, Mortie could see that the room was very large and that there were many people here; in fact, he could not see the end of them.

They crossed the courtyard. It was a strange experience, at least to Mortie, since he loved books and somehow had conceived of writers as convivial people. But none of the writers looked up or expressed the least interest in the passing people; instead they kept staring at their computers or, in one case, seemed to be scribbling frantically and tearing at a long legal pad.

“So these are all writers?” said Mortie, looking with interest at the people. They all seem a little preoccupied….”

“Well, they are… But they’re the best,” said Beatrice. “Every one of our people is at least edit-quality people.”

“Edit quality…?”

“Even better,” she said. “Some of them…”

They continued on. In front of them, to the right as you entered the courtyard, was a large, glass, walled atrium.”

“This is one of our exercise rooms,” said Beatrice. They peered in. The room was completely enclosed in glass. In the room, there didn’t seem to be anything but two large pools with several huge logs floating therein.

Blackie rubbed at the glass, trying to see in better. "Are those logs?" he exclaimed.

"Yes of course," said Beatrice. "Watch, now…."

Soon two people clambered onto the log with amazing agility. They began turning the log under their feet, slowly, and then faster, spinning the log under their feet.

"What is it?" said Blackie with astonishment, and no small amount of envy, since he very much admired anyone with great dexterity.

"Log rolling. It's their favorite thing to do…."

"Log rolling?"

"Yes…. The writers groups especially love it," she said. "You can't keep them from it. It's great exercise and they do it all the time…."

But just then, one of the log rollers made a misstep and tumbled awkwardly into the pool, banging an arm painfully against the spinning log. She disappeared into the water. There were bubbles.

"Oh man!" said Mortie anxious for the woman to come up. "Should we help? She might be hurt. I can go in there…"

"Not to worry," exclaimed Beatrice laughing heartily. "She's *fiiin*e…. These writers love a little pain."

And it was true, for the now swimming writer had clambered out of the pool, grinning broadly, while rubbing a wound on her arm that was only bleeding slightly. Meanwhile, the writer still on the log had, by amazing dexterity with her tap dancing feet, slowed the extreme spin rate of the log. When the log's spin was slowed almost to a stop, she danced lightly along the log, and caused it to move toward the verge of the pool, where another log rolling writer was waiting in line to step on."

"They're all waiting to get on?"

"Oh, they live for it," said Beatrice. "We're never short of log rollers."

"They're all writers?"

"Well, poets mostly…" said Beatrice. "These are the best poets in the country."

"Wow," said Mortie, very impressed.

"You can't even get in here unless you've won a grant. We try to take care of them. They love the log stuff. Some of them recite while they're spinning. They get clean, too, if they fall." She chuckled. "Those scamps don't really like to shower or bathe a lot, so the pool is a life saver, especially for the rest of us. It saves time."

"I had no idea this was in our city," said Blackie, as they were passing a paneled room with a lot of men and women around a table.

"We have a publishing section here…" she said. "That is a meeting of our editors."

The people in the meeting were smiling broadly.

"They seem happy…" said Mortie.

"They should be," she said. "They're paid to do it. They're all former English teachers…."

"Are they writers?"

"Oh no, they don't have to be able to write. They're editors…!" She pointed excitedly down a dark hallway. "There he is! Mr. Preshion," she yelled.

"Who?" said Mortie.

"Camrok D. Preshion," she said. "He is America's best writer now."

"The best?"

"Bar none. He's so good he never gives interviews."

"That makes him good?" said Blackie, who really had little opinion on the subject.

"Oh yes…!" she said, frowning at such an absurd question.

"And he comes here?" said Mortie. "Why…?"

I don't know what Mortie was expecting, but Preshion was a disappointment. He was old, and tiny, and bent, his face lined. The fingers of one hand appeared cramped and knotted as though he had been at some manual labor for most of his life. His eyes darted about and were rheumy and bloodshot and bulged, making him look like a border lizard trying to decide between eating another bug or avoiding the sun. What other expression they contained was distant and distrustful.

"Senevitch…?" mused Preshion in response to their question.

"Did you know him?" said Mortie.

"Know him? What happened?"

"He was found in the park," said Blackie. "He is deceased."

At this D. Preshion seemed to shake off a dream and grow more aware. He made a small inquiring gesture with his hand.

"How?"

Blackie looked at Mortie. "He was killed, we think. Do you know anything about him?"

D. Preshion seemed to lighten. "Shot, perhaps…?" he said, looking at them hopefully. "Gouts of blood…, torn celeopotric eruptions…"

"What?" exclaimed Blackie, startled by this response from so benign looking an old man. "No blood…. Quite clean, actually. Pale, though. He was found by the river in Riverside Park…. We're just running leads down, sir. Did you…"

"Harried, hour by hour," interrupted D. Preshion in a low voice. "Driven with violent self-wrought flailing to the river, he slept uneasily along the grassy verge in switchgrass, alder and willow, muttering and moaning, curled, like a dog, rotten and rank boots steaming in the ashes of the self-built fire, twitching like a discalced penitent. In the night, the mists settled on him, inchoate and silvery.

"Ummm… I don't know… said Blackie. "Fires aren't allowed in the park."

"So, you know he was wet?" said Mortie, who didn't want to interrupt so prominent a man, but saw no other option, considering. "What else?"

"Virgo and Sagittarius rose, and the men rose," said D. Preshion. "…as all men rise, from some desecrated venal scoring of earth, slavering, eyes glowing, lit by an unknowable, filial fire, essence drained from some remembered primal volcanic heat."

"Look," said Blackie impatiently. "Do you know him? We have a book of matches with your name on it and the telephone number of this place. We don't have a lot to go on, but…?"

But D. Preshion was walking toward a dark place down the hall, his hand twitching.

"What a man," said Beatrice in awe.

Blackie watched Preshion go. "Cheerful, ain't he? Should I go get him?"

"He lives on a lower level," Celia said. "Do you want to follow him?"

"There's a lower level?" said Mortie.

"Several," said Beatrice.

"I think not… Just now, that is. Perhaps later, at least in my case. I'm not sure about my partner."

They did not have to decide, in any case, since Beatrice apparently had had enough of this, and hustled them through a door… which somehow led outside. They stood blinking in intense sunlight. Amazingly, they were on the street where they had started with their squad car.

"You've finally done it," said Blackie, after they had recovered their vision and were driving away.

"What…?"

"That was without a doubt the dumbest, weirdest thing you've ever gotten me into…."

Mortie was wheeling through traffic. He laughed suddenly.

"What…?"

"Have you ever thought that *we* just might be characters in a book…"

"What?" said Blackie again.

"…Manipulated by some idiot with a pen and some paper."

"Not a chance," said Blackie who was, after all, the ultimate realist.

Eleven

"Mortimer…! How enjoyable to see you! How is your dear mother?" exclaimed Johnson, an avuncular, portly man, who, it seemed, was permanently and happily welded to a chair in Administration.

Blackie was gone, huddled over in Captain Groatly's office. "Systems analysis…" he said, when they met for lunch one day. He took a bite of a foot-long Subway sandwich at lunch. "Cross analyzing crime statistics, distribution, location, et cetera, integrating and coordinating same with written department and interdepartmental policy."

Mortie, feeling dislocated without his partner, threw himself into his work, at least existentially. He woke early, grabbed a coffee, and worked all day alone. One day, he wandered the cubicle warrens of the city.

The flicker of a cloud passed across Johnson's eyes, an almost imperceptible shifting of his body, when Mortie described the information he thought he'd like to access for the investigation.

"I'd *love* to get you that information," Johnson said.

"Oh good….," said Mortie. "I thought it might be harder – knowing the regs these days."

"Of course I'd have to talk with my Department head."

"Oh…?"

"And… run it by IDRC…."

"Rules…?"

"The Interdepartmental Rules Committee," nodded Johnson, giving Mortie a knowing look. "As we say, "There are rules and there's Rules…."

"So how long…?"

"And, of course there's Legal…. "*You,* of all people, know how *touchy* they can be…."

"Undoubtedly," said Mortie. "So how long…?"

Johnson smiled generously. "Well, for starters… Let's see… I *am* extraordinarily busy this month… I'd have to get up a memorandum… at the very minimum."

"A memorandum," said Mortie. "Is a memorandum necessary?"

Johnson frowned, this time with all of the certainty that a memorandum brings. "Necessary…? My dear Mortimer, I would never make a move without one…."

"And the purpose of it would be?" said Mortie, who was beginning to be impatient with all of this "dear Mortimer"-ing.

"To circulate, of course…," said Johnson firmly, shifting his considerable weight around on his seat.

"You circulate something like a request for some data?"

Johnson seemed intensely unhappy with this unfortunate reality of modern bureaucratic life. "Yesterday, I would have slammed something together and out the door." He made an abrupt sliding motion with his right hand. "Just like that…."

"And now…?"

"Times have changed…" said Johnson sadly. "What with the rash of poaching and all."

"Poaching…?"

"The unfortunate habit of raiding departmental purviews. Department personell trying to grab responsibilities across interdepartmental lines…" Johnson frowned. "It's an epidemic. Every time there's budget stress, we get a lot more of it. Everyone wants to increase their reach now…. Poaching… a very bad business. Puts one on edge."

"So how long to write the…?"

"And…" said Johnson, interrupting Mortie and holding up a finger. "I would have to have something in writing from you."

"From me…?"

"A request, of course…."

"You don't really want to do anything, do you, Johnson?"

"*Nonsense*!" exclaimed Johnson. "I am shocked you would say such a thing, my dear Mortimer. Of course we *want* to cooperate with you. But look… Just send me a little something…covering all of the salient points, of course. And be patient. It takes a while…."

"I guess," said Mortie getting up to go.

"We *must* do lunch sometime…" said Johnson as Mortie wandered away through the cubicles. "I *do* so admire your mother…."

Early evening. Mortie ate at a sweaty truck stop diner, south on Wilshere Blvd. On the counter was sugar in pour containers instead of those little packets, and the food came clicking and clattering through the steel window from the kitchen. The waitresses were skinny, and fat, and middling, and they joked, and frowned, and yelled, and laughed with each other. The one that served him had a stain on the front of her dress, and a mass of jangling jewelry on her wrists, and a tiny gold cross hanging around her neck… and she called him "Honey." He watched the people come in… blown in off the windy freeway. There were fat-bellied truckers and hot-faced salesman, and construction workers in sweat-stained, torn tee-shirts. There were cops and there were business guys in from their glass cages. There were bureaucrats and long distance people… coast-to-coasters, twitchy from the road, with empty, placid eyes, like new-born babies.

Night found him parked on a busy street, waiting. For a few seconds, he thought of Filthy Phil Muldoon, the legendary undercover expert. (Showers once a week, lives on stakeouts and takeout. When he undercovers, no squirrel is safe around him. Alas, he does not appear in this story.) He watched a man walking down the street. The man's head was on a swivel, looking this way and that, sometimes glancing into cars. Normal people don't swivel like that. The man stopped and stared back down the street. He turned and hurried into a Salvation Army store. In a moment, a patrol car rolled by. A car-crasher, maybe. Mortie watched the cars, ruminating upon the fact that it is hard to see someone sitting in a car in daylight even a half block away. A normal person doesn't think of such things. Criminals and cops think that way.

Two women walked past.

"He takes his temperature every two hours, for god's sake…!" said the willowy one."

"Why…?"

"He thinks he has a fever…."

"Does he?"

"It's 98.6 every time…."

"Well…" said the other woman. "At least he's not fooling around…"

"I wish he would fool around more. First, it was blood pressure, now this! Christ, the man's crazy as a loon."

"As a loon?"

"It's an expression. I used to live in… Oh, never mind."

The sun sank, exhausted, into the western hills. There was a song on the radio. *You build it up and you tear it down, you burn the mansion to the ground.* He thought of Gloria. A sadness… but for no reason. A fog rolled in. Mortie was watching a street corner. In a while, a man came from the darkness, meandered into the pool of light under the street light, and leaned into a shadow that clung to a building. There was a flare, and then a pinpoint glow. Mortie put on his trench coat and walked over.

"You Bruckner?"

The man blew a stream of smoke. “Yes… I’m Bruckner…”

“Anton…?”

Bruckner examined his cigarette. “Don’t start…”

“Get a lot of that, do you?”

“Only from the classical music freaks like you.”

“Is it that apparent?” said Mortie.

“I can spot ‘em a mile off…”

“Tough…”

Bruckner’s voice became a tremolo “Know this tune, Bruckner?” he whined. “Hum a few bars, Bruckner. Seen Wagner lately, Bruckner? Compose yourself, Bruckner. Why do you think I hang around the night crowd, Jablonsky? At least most of them can’t carry a tune.”

“So you’re not a…”

Bruckner’s voice rose; an octave, Mortie thought. “I’m a painter.”

“Oh good!” said Mortie, who loved art. “What sort are you? Impressionist, Post Moder…”

“Houses…. And I hate music. What can I do for you, Jablonsky.”

“You know Jackson, I hear.”

“I knew him some…”

“Knew him? Is he…”

Bruckner took a drag on his cigarette. “Left town a year ago, best I figure… He was here and then wasn’t….”

“Was he involved in the drug business?”

"Small time shit.... He always had a kilo or two around. Part time money..."

"Nothing else...?"

"Nothing that I know of. I think he went back to Texas. He was always talkin' about how great the gulf fishing was down there."

"There's a woman involved with the dope business..." said Mortie as calmly and with as much authority as he could muster.

Bruckner looked at him and then smiled faintly. "You don't know, do you?"

Mortie said nothing. A siren wailed somewhere. Bruckner shifted and looked around uneasily.

"I hear something about a woman. Look I gotta get go..."

"You seen Kiriov...?"

"The Russian?"

"Yes..."

"Not much." Bruckner fumbled in his jacket. "Why don't you try that moldy dump he peddles books out of...?"

"Did. Hasn't been there much...."

"He's there most of the time," said Bruckner, his voice changing tempo. "You just have to wait him out. He thinks that crap is worth a mint.... It's a fire trap. They'll find him dead in there some time."

"Where else...?"

Bruckner lit another cigarette. "He thinks he's a music expert. I stay away from him. I hear he's been at the

Stardust. He thinks he's a reviewer. Some jazz trio." He started walking away and then stopped and looked back. "Look, I'll call if I get a name on a woman. And then we're even. No more."

"Stardust? Isn't that on…" started Mortie eagerly.

Bruckner sighed. He nodded. "Ninth and…" He grimaced at Mortie. "You people never quit, do you…?"

When he was gone, Mortie took a plastic bag from his pocket, walked over, picked up one of Bruckner's cigarette butts, and put it into the bag.

People had once lined up to get in the Stardust Lounge. These days, the place looked as if anyone in their right mind would line up to get out. There was music, though. A piano trio had crowded onto a little stage and was lurching through an interpretation of Fats Waller's *Ain't Misbehavin*. There was a haze layer in the air. At the Stardust, the patrons did not seem to care a fig for memoranda, committees, or regulations of any sort, particularly smoking regulations.

"They want to smoke," wheezed Pops, the owner. "Let them, I say. Maybe I get closed down. What's the hell's the difference…?" He whipped a towel over his shoulder. "I'm seventy five years old. I can't even break up a fight any more." He pointed to a mountainous chunk of flesh trying to tip over the bar by leaning on it. "I got to get C. H. over there to do it for me."

"Hell of a deal," said Mortie. "Kiriov been in…?"

"Over there," Pops said, pointing to a dark skinned, sharply angular man sitting in a shadowy alcove. "Goddamn Russian… Buys one beer and talks to his friends on that damned phone for two hours. I hate cell phones."

"You do…?"

"Got live music. Sometimes they get in tune. And so what happens? The goddamn phones go off right in the middle, and some guy starts yelling into his phone about his girlfriend… or his trip to the Grand Canyon. And the louder the music, the louder he yells. Never seen the like of it. Tell him to buy a drink every now and then."

The trio started into an approximation of a famous jazz tune. Kiriov was sitting at a tiny triangular table. The alcove had a small slit window, very coated with grime and dust, so that only a faint yellowish light made it through to the table. The alcove, though tiny, had once been ornate. Somewhere along the line, someone had pasted various beer advertisements and a few pennants on the wall. One of the pennants was not for beers, but instead had once advertised a fish monger's shop. It had once been red, but smoke and dirt and time had made it brown, and also scratched and peeled in places, so that all that could be made out were the words *Fre h Herring*.

Mortie went over. Kiriov barely glanced up. He was so thin he seemed as though he might fold up like an empty suit of clothes. Most of the time, he watched the two men and the drunken woman try to perform jazz on the tiny stage. From time to time, he glanced intently at a chess board. He had a sour expression on his face. Apparently, the trio wasn't performing to his satisfaction… or this was the regular expression of Russian expats. He was smoking with a considered intensity, as though this cigarette might be the last he would ever have.

"Hello, Kiriov," said Mortie.

Kiriov pointed to a chair, and Mortie sat.

"What did he say?" said Kiriov.

"He said how much he likes Russians."

"Old bastard," said Kiriov without rancor. He nodded at the bar. "Want to bet on whether she'll fall off the stage?"

Mortie turned toward the stage for a moment. "Maybe better for the music."

Kiriov sighed and arranged some pieces on the chess board. The smoke curled up into his eyes, causing him to squint at the arrangement of chess men; or chess *persons*, if you like. He took off some wire-rimmed glasses, rubbed them a little on his shirt, and put them back. He squinted at Mortie.

"I'm supposed to be writing a review of them."

"Are you going to…?"

"Maybe… They won't like it, so maybe I shouldn't. Want a game?"

Mortie laughed. "A good high school kid could beat me. I don't think I'm at your level."

"In that case," said Kiriov. "What do you want?"

"Oh, I don't know. How's business?"

“I peddle used books,” said Kiriov. “People bring in their paperbacks. I resell them. I get a lot of people who want to spend nickels. I make enough to pay the bills and hang around places like this. How great could it be?”

“You get along… And you get around a lot at night.”

Kiriov hunched forward and moved a piece on his board. “Every snipe likes his own swamp.”

“Mortie laughed. “A Russian saying, isn’t it? You like these places.”

“Singers… It’s a weakness. Remind me of my mother.”

“Your mother?”

“Big, black, beautiful Vera. An actress. A socialist. A union activist. She could have been great on TV. McCarthy showed up. She was an easy target. Ever hear of the List?”

“No….”

“A list went around. Names… She suddenly couldn’t get TV work. Sang in the clubs. Lot of good it did. They got along until the government threatened the clubs. No more of that.”

“Your father…?”

“Anatov Kiriov, professional failure… Sucker for a cause…” He waved his cigarette. “He wrote pamphlets…, organizing tracts.” He sucked hard on his cigarette. “I live off him. He liked collecting old books. The neighborhood is a dump now. Maybe I’ll sell them when I dump this place and move to Mexico. The only thing that keeps my books safe is that the thieves don’t have a clue as to what’s valuable and what isn’t.”

"He left Russia…?"

Kiriov shrugged. "No one leaves Russia…."

"Where…?"

"The Steppes… Intellectuals… Russia is full of them. Bad roads, great composers, and an intellectual behind every bush. Stalin didn't mind the roads, and he tolerated a few of the composers, but he didn't trust intellectuals."

"Why…?"

Kiriov smiled vaguely. "Because they think too much…. Then they get too big for their britches."

"Quite the story…."

"Sure… A thrill a minute…" said Kiriov bleakly. "A black woman socialist and a white Russian. That was going to turn out great. Ended up destitute, selling books on street corners." Afterward, mother moved here and bought this place." Kiriov looked up. "I won't end up like that."

"No…" said Mortie. "I don't suppose."

"I asked you what you wanted."

You ever heard of a woman who sells dope around?"

Kiriov looked at him. "Name?"

"Don't have a name…"

"Can't help then…"

"Senevitch…?"

Kiriov looked up. "I heard something about him. In the park?"

"That's right…."

Kiriov shifted in his seat uncomfortably. He sucked harder on his cigarette. "I talk to a lot of people. I can't say I remember him. He wasn't a player."

"You can't say?"

Something in Kiriov's expression went sullen. "I don't remember him."

"A guy named Jackson…?"

"Never heard of him. I'm a business owner. That's all. Look, Jablonsky," Kiriov said, pointing at the bandstand where the trio were somehow sounding better. "They might never get in tune again." He looked intently at Mortie suddenly. "What the hell do you think you're doing…?"

Mortie was taken aback… "What do you mean?"

"You're fishing in old, dirty water, Jablonsky…."

"I don't get it…."

Kiriov shook his head. "Look, when Blighe went down and then… years ago when your… when Powell came in…"

"Yes…?"

"Well, everything changed. When Blighe went down, he took some others with him. It was a hell of a mess. Your uncle smoothed it all over. He did a good job…."

"And…?"

"And they just left it like that."

"So… I don't get it."

"So politicians don't get elected by raising a lot of furor. They wanted it out of the way. They wanted the bodies to stay buried, so to speak."

"And the dope market?"

"That's the point.... Somebody smart took over."

"Who?"

"I don't know..." said Kiriov, moving a piece on the chessboard. "But I know one thing."

"What's that...?"

"It's somebody who doesn't like trouble; doesn't want trouble, and doesn't like publicity. He's a pro.... A pro knows that sort of thing is bad for business. Anyway, there were casualties. Really innocent people got taken down.

"Before my time... Who?"

Kiriov shook his head again. "Are you sure you want to get into this?"

"I don't know if I have a choice..."

Kiriov smiled bitterly at this response. "The others figured out their choices...."

"Who got taken down..?"

"Well, there's a lot of talk that Overbight's partner was set up."

"What happened?"

"He was killed. I don't know for sure. He was shot in some sort of a bust."

"Was he set up...?"

Kiriov shrugged. "I doubt it.... It probably was a matter of bad luck."

"Bad luck...? How so...?"

Kiriov laughed bitterly. "Wrong place. Wrong time. No backup, I hear. Bad luck. A bullet.... Dead...."

"Are they all dead...?"

“Mostly… Retired, dead, and gone….” Kiriov paused.

“What?”

“Captain Dickerson is still around somewhere, I hear…. Might as well be dead. Christ, ask your boss…”

“I’d rather ask you,” said Mortie. “Captain Dickerson is still around?”

Kiriov took a drag on his cigarette. “Lot of good that will do. He won’t talk…. Unlisted phone, I hear. Doesn’t go out. Hasn’t for years….”

“Did you ever tell all of this to anyone…?”

Kiriov looked up. He smirked. “In the first place, why the hell would I volunteer anything? And in the second place, no one asked.”

“No one?”

Kiriov turned back to the board. “Nyet, comrade…. I don’t think they wanted to find out.”

Mortie got up. “You know Kline…?”

Kiriov’s face slowly turned up to Mortie again. “What about him?”

“I hear he hangs around a place south…”

“I don’t get it. He’s a cop. You’re a cop. Ask him yourself.”

“Don’t want to. I’d like to just show up.”

“The Longhorn. 50th and 4th … Bunch of cowboys.”

Mortie got up.

“They don’t like cops down there,” said Kiriov suddenly.

“What about Kline? He’s a cop.”

Kiriov smirked. “They like him. They’re afraid of him.”

Mortie was in his car. He dialed a number. “Mother…?”

The phone rang and rang. He hung up. Almost immediately, his phone rang. “Mortimer? Was that you, dear? Are you okay…?”

“What…? Yes, of course. Why?”

“Well, for one thing, it’s eleven at night….”

“Oh crap…” exclaimed Mortie.

“Don’t swear, Mortimer. It’s so…”

“Sorry, Mother. I just got caught up in something and forgot what time it was…. I can call back in the morning….”

“Oh no… No… It’s okay. I was up, anyway. What’s up?”

“When you were at the city, you knew Captain Dickerson?”

A long silence. “Yes… What about him…?”

“Nothing much. I’m running down something and I need to talk with him.”

“He won’t talk….”

“So I hear…. Can you try…?” Another pause. “Mother?”

“I’m thinking…. Are you sure you should get involved in this?”

“No… But I have to find out some things….”

“May I call you back, dear?”

“Of course… I’m up late….”

"I can't guarantee anything, Mortimer."
"No problem."
"It probably will be late morning."

Mortie sat on a bench in a small green park late the next morning. The sun had dried the dew. He had stopped for a coffee at an upscale coffee shop in a shopping center. The coffee in this place was watery. Still, it *was* upscale. Two men in front of him were having trouble deciding which pastries to buy. They stood, and stood, debating. The lady at the cash register smiled. She had been smiling like this for two years. All that smiling had permanently fixed that smile on her face.

"It all looks so good heh, heh," said one of the men. "I can't decide between the Cranberry Orange Muffin and the Incredibly Amazing Breakfast Muffin." He was a man of about fifty years old with silver hair. He was wearing shorts made of some glossy silky material... and sandals. The fabric of the shorts outlined his butt cheeks. There ought to be some rule against fifty-year-old men wearing flimsy shorts in the morning.

"Look at the Craisin Almond Scone," said his friend. The men stood there admiring the pastries.

In order to distract himself from the urge to squeeze one of their heads until the brain popped out, Mortie began staring at the man's toenails. The man had the best looking toenails he had ever seen. He had to give him that. Especially for a man of his age, although, to be honest,

Mortie was unsure of the effect of age on toenails. He based it all on his grandmother's nails, which he had once seen. A nasty sight.

In any case, these weren't like that. These were *great* toenails. Each was formed perfectly, trimmed and clear. People would kill for such toenails. He thought with slight embarrassment of his own mangled and twisted toenails. And he was only in his twenties. He felt that way, although no one could actually see his nails. He resolved to take better care of them. He was going to say something complimentary to the man about his toenails; after all they had been standing together in front of the pastry display for quite a long while. He decided not to, though. It wasn't the type of thing you say much about. When it was finally his turn, he ordered a medium Mocha to go. Remembering the wateriness of previous versions from this place, he had them add a shot of espresso; only a dollar more.

It was warm in the park now. The coffee had been too hot at first, and was perfect now, so he was sipping, and listening to the city, and watching people. He liked this bench. There was a plaque on the bench. A nice bench with a plaque. The plaque was brass, and small, and worn, with an inscription. He liked this bench. He did not know who had put the plaque there, and he could not read the inscription, and somehow that was comforting. He had gotten used to the plaque, and paid it little notice these days, but he still liked the fact that it was there when he came here. He took a sip and watched a jogger. He did not often see people that he knew here. Since his days as a patrolman, Mortie had found it very settling in his mind to occasionally just walk around parts of the city. This was a favorite place to sit and listen and watch.

Two nuns came by. They were gesturing and talking animatedly. They nodded to Mortie, but stopped talking while in his hearing range.

A huge dog pulling a little man came in from the street. The dog lunged toward an elm tree and, as if elms hadn't enough trouble, commenced sniffing eagerly at its base.

"Gerald…" said the man, tugging on the leash. The huge dog braced its feet and continued sniffing.

"Gerald…" the man said. "Gerald."

Gerald ignored him, rooted to the spot…. "Come on, Gerald…. Gerald…" Finally, Gerald, having exhausted the inventory of dogs who'd visited that same tree, figured he'd had enough and lifted his leg. When he was done, he started dragging the little man toward another a tree further down the jogging path.

"Wait, Gerald…" implored the man. "Wait…"

Two young women hurried along the path, talking and gesturing, one tall and slightly gangly, and the other fireplug short. Mortie vaguely recognized the taller one, and she glanced at him.

"Omygod," said one. "I was like, *why* would you say that?"

"You did?'

"And you know what he said?"

"No, what…?"

"Omygod it's..."

"What!"

"He said, because he thinks… Like… I'm v*ain*… Can you believe that?"

"Ooooh."

"Like LOL… *I'm* vain…. He's vain, if you ask me…"

A man sat on a bench across the path, nodded to Mortie, and took a coffee and a donut out of a paper bag.

Mortie sipped his coffee and scanned through his paper for a while, finding nothing of interest, save the comics. A woman jogged the path, dressed in slightly more than she had worn into the shower that morning, plus running shoes, sun glasses, and ear phones, for privacy. Both Mortie and the man across the path looked up. She slowed a little, scowled at them, and jogged off toward downtown, where there were more people to ignore.

His phone chimed.

"He'll see you at three o'clock," his mother said. "I'd be on time if I were you…."

Twelve

Dickerson lived at the end of a short driveway that curved downhill through an old patch of ironwood and basswood. Dogwood grew ten feet high on both sides. The driveway had jolting potholes that no one had touched in any way. Dickerson's rambler was brighter than he expected. Bright swatches of flowers in small gardens grew around the house. A woman was waiting for him in the portico.

"He has Alzheimer's…" she said.

Mortie stopped. This had never occurred to him. Of all of the possibilities…. "I don't have to do this," he said. "I can go…"

She shrugged. "No… no… It's okay. It's not advanced…. He likes to talk sometimes." She gestured toward the back of the house.

Dickerson was small and wiry-looking and was dressed in ancient khakis. He had a garden trowel in one hand and a large hat in the other. He watched Mortie.

"Thanks for letting me…" began Mortie, but the little man ignored him and gestured toward a deck.

"Come this way. I'm about ready to have my jolt for the day." There was a large deck overlooking a ravine. "I usually have two, one here and one with my dinner." He looked up at Mortie. "She says I knew your mother. You're a big one, aren't you…?"

Dickerson began to pour each of them a drink from a pitcher. "Try that," said Dickerson.

Mortie sipped the martini. It tasted like something that might come out of a blow torch. He tried to think of some way to start.

Dickerson sat watching him. His eyes were very bright. "So, what's on your mind?" he said. "Unless this is purely social. In which case, drink up…."

"We, that is, my partner and I, were…"

"Who's that?"

"John Blackman. He's…"

"Never heard of him. So you're police?"

"Detective…"

"I was a cop once…" said Dickerson.

Mortie wondered if he should just leave. "Yes… That's why I'm here. When Blighe… left, you were working a drug task force…"

Dickerson stared at him. "Yes, Blighe… That's right…."

"What happened?"

"What do you mean, 'what happened?'"

"Were you making any progress?"

Dickerson got out a pack of cigarettes. His hands shook a little, and he frowned and hid them, as though this irritated him. He lit a cigarette, shook the match out, and tossed it off the deck. "I like to smoke," he said, as though to himself. "They say I've got the goddamned Alzheimer's."

"You seem pretty good to me…."

Dickerson laughed. "Yeah, bullshit…. It's odd. I remember some things at a go. Things twenty years ago. Or when I was a kid. Then some days… nothing."

"You were on the Drug Task Force."

Dickerson nodded. "DTF Three…. I was on DTF Sector Three… Blessing was our squad leader. We didn't really have a good handle on it all… We had some guys in mind… They screwed us!" he suddenly yelled at Mortie.

"Who screwed you?"

"Who? Who the hell do you think? All of them, goddamn them all. They got Blighe."

"I thought Blighe was caught in…?"

Dickerson shrugged. "A goddamn drunk, okay, I know. Sloppy as a shit pail full of fish, all right. They knew it, too… Set him up…."

Mortie suddenly felt weak. "A setup…?"

"Blighe was a drunk, but he was hell on drugs. He supported us all the way."

"And after…?"

"Nothing… The druggies got a new boss, we heard. Whoever it was leaned on every snitch. Not a ripple on the water. When there were deliveries after that, we heard about them later. It was like they were reading our minds."

"Did you think they might have had inside information?"

Dickerson eyed him for a moment. "Of course… Do you think we didn't know anything…?"

"So…?"

"So people started to be suspicious of each other…. And that wasn't the worst of it."

"What happened then?"

Dickerson looked like a man in an empty room looking for something. "Rumors… Rumors…! One after the other."

What sort of rumors?"

"I don't know… Dope missing from evidence. Rotten cop rumors. Drug task force rumors. Beating up people rumors. A little here and a little there. Powell really had no choice then… It went on for months."

"So my uncle dismantled the task force…?"

"The unit got reorganized. People shifted around."

"Blessing?"

"Blessing…?"

"He was killed," prompted Mortie.

"Who are you?" said Dickerson pointing a finger at him.

"Jablonsky, sir. I'm a detective. Blessing?"

"Oh, right… I knew your mother. Blessing…. Him and Overbight were off the task force. Working chop. Bunch of shit. But Blessing didn't quit. He must have found some string to the affair there. He found some new snitches. The Asians didn't like all the drug stuff because they had a good deal going in autos."

"Theft?"

"Parts…. More money chopping….. The drug outfit started sending drugs in auto part shipments. Blessing got onto it."

"And…? Did anything come of it…?"

"Blessing wouldn't talk. He didn't trust anyone. I don't blame him. I don't think he even told his partner. He is working some deal."

"He's dead, sir…."

"Dead…? Dead, dead." laughed Dickerson. "Yes, I heard that. Anything can happen when they drop the dime. You just have to assume every time they aren't safe. You have to have your partner there."

Mortie could not think of a thing to say. "Overbight?"

"He was all right," said Dickerson. "Is he dead too?"

"No. He's…"

"Powell tried to cover for him. Did what he could. But what-the-jesus-h-christ could he do? He was busy. Talk, talk, talk."

"Let me guess," said Mortie. "Someone was saying he was in on his partner's murder."

"What…? Yeah…" Dickerson suddenly shrunk into a long silence. Then – "That about fixed his ass…. You don't have to shoot someone to kill them off." Dickerson pointed his finger at Mortie. "Let me give you some advice, young man. Get off your butt. Hit the streets… Footwork…! That's the way to solve this thing."

"Yes, sir… That is essential to good police work. We do have a few tools that weren't… available when you…."

Dickerson suddenly seemed to shrink more, defeated by something he could not name…. "I hope… I hope you get them…" he murmured.

"Let me make you a promise, sir," Mortie said quietly, getting to his feet. "You can rest your mind about that. Because we are going to get them…. You can take that to the bank."

The woman was waiting in the portico. She nodded toward a large box. "This was from… those days," she said. She crossed her arms. "I was just going to throw it away."

"What is it?"

"I don't know. Stuff from work back then." She turned to go back into the house. "He took it home because he didn't trust anyone."

He was pulling away again when his cell phone buzzed.

"This is Melissa Perlsworth…. We should meet…" she said.

Thirteen

Mortie thought he'd found the wrong place. The coffee shop to which she had given him the address was far out in an upscale suburban shopping center. Across the parking lot, a poodle was demonstrating how he had perfectly trained his master, a thin, expensive-looking blonde, to hold out a cup for him while he debated whether to drink or not from it. This time, the poodle was seeing how long it could get the woman to hold the cup. Occasionally, the poodle lowered his head, taking a sip. The poodle took a sip and winked at Mortie. In the coffee shop, a large Mexican man sitting in the corner nodded at him and then began whispering something that Mortie could not understand.

Three expensively dressed women sat in a corner of the room. A couple took a table in back of him. "You do it," said one of the two. "You have to learn to do for yourself," said a woman's voice behind him. The man returned to the table, carrying two donuts and two coffees. Mortie was reading a local newspaper. "Well?" said the woman.

"It's only a donut…!" said the man.

"Say it…" hissed the woman.

"Aw…"

"George…!"

"Oh, fine.... Thank you, Jesus for these… donuts."

Mortie turned to look at the couple. A woman stared, pursed-mouth, back at him. The faintest expression of triumph ran around her face and disappeared into that mouth.

There was a man in the street wearing cargo pants, tennis shoes, and a sweatshirt. He was laughing and gesturing. Too much coffee. His laugh reminded Mortie of a machine gun. "Ahahahahahaha, he laughed. "Ahahahahaha…"

Melissa Perlsworth came hurrying in.

She was wearing a rose-colored blouse, a scarf, and slacks. Her lips were full and faintly red. Her eyes were a hazel blue. She moved… somehow quickly, but seemingly with no haste. People gaped. The women gaped. Mortie gaped.

"Hi…" she said.

She sipped tea and gazed at him with very large, calm eyes that would suddenly become very slightly disturbed, as if reflecting a sunny day, but with a storm off on the horizon. Mortie had to remind himself that she was at least forty years old.

And he was the cop.

She smiled with that same, faintly amused expression that he had noticed the first time they had met. *I know men. I like men. It's fun!* – the expression said. She sipped tea. Her lips were a shade of faint red. She licked them.

"I'm not sure of exactly how to start…"

"Just start," said Mortie. How long have you run the coffee house?"

"Oh… the last year and a half…. My husband died eight years ago…"

"Sorry…."

"For a number of years, I couldn't do much. But then I got myself together, and the chance to open the store came along. Wicca helps. Life and death are a natural process to us." She considered him. "And I want you to understand that we do not ask who is at our convocations. And further, in our history, that is Wicca history, the use of drugs like marijuana was not unusual."

"So…?"

"So, our group is not involved in the movement and sale of any drugs. The use of marijuana in our history is debatable. In other words, some say these drugs and various psychedelics were used; usually only by the Shamans." She considered Mortie. "And in my group, we do not allow that…. I would not have my group involved in any drugs."

"Is someone accusing you of it?"

"That's not it. And I don't know anything about that unfortunate man they found in the park."

Some interesting perfume… like the smell of Orchids… reached him.

"So?"

"So…" she paused. "One of our people is involved with drugs. At least, I think so."

"Who is it…?"

"I don't know…."

"You don't know…?"

"A woman, is all that I know…."

"How do you know that anything is going on…?"

"I don't know for sure," she said. Her hands began gesturing in the most graceful way. She looked straight into his eyes. "But as you know, we conduct our services very early in the mornings. That's to be sure we will be there at sunrise."

"And…?"

"On one occasion, one of our people – someone who usually drives over to the services – parked and walked over through those buildings on the north end of the park, near the grow buildings."

Her eyes had changed to a slightly darker blue. She watched some cars on the street. Her blouse fell open a little. A little light fell on the cream white curve of her breast. Mortie swallowed.

"She saw some men come out of the buildings. They were in a hurry. They had a lot of small packages. She did not think much of it. After all, the parks workers get going pretty early."

"And…?" croaked Mortie.

"And she stopped to watch. They didn't see her. They were hurrying. They left in a van.

"And…?"

"She thought she recognized one of them. A short woman, who had been to our services…."

"Did she know the name of the woman?"

"No… As I say…"

"Stocky?" said Mortie.

"I asked that… The word she used was 'short'…. Hard to say in the dark.

"And then?"

"And so then in their hurrying, one of them dropped one of the packages and another of them stepped on it. Or something…. Anyway, they gathered up the packages and left. When they were gone, she got curious as to why they were in so much of a hurry. She saw a white spot on the ground. So she gathered it up and put it in a bag. There was this…"

She opened her handbag, retrieved two paperback books, and set them aside on the table. The books were much read and used. The cover of one of the paperbacks was cracked slightly and curled back. Someone had scrawled a telephone number on an inside page and then thoroughly crossed it out. Mortie idly held the page to the light. He could make out the last four digits: 4002.

"You like to read?" he asked.

"Of course… she said, rummaging around in her bag. "Eye candy, mostly. Fluff… Used books, mostly. I get them at a used book store."

"Kiriov's?"

She smiled. "Yes… He's good. And cheap." She retrieved a bag that contained some whitish powder and dirt, and handed it to Mortie.

Mortie looked. He wet his finger and gingerly tasted the contents.

"Can you tell if it's cocaine, doing that…?"

"No… I just saw this on a cop show," said Mortie. "It has to go to the lab. It could be anything…"

She nodded. "True, and it could be something…"

"Why are you telling me this?"

She reached over and touched his arm. "Because I do not want our religion sullied, Lieutenant."

"Will you call me if you hear any more?" he said. His tongue seemed to stick to the roof of his mouth when he talked to her.

She slowly smiled. "I will…." She rose and left. People watched.

He wheeled down Central toward the south of the city, feeling slightly unhinged. He had the awful feeling that she could ask anything of him, and he'd do it. "She even likes books," he thought. He imagined them walking together. He imagined them……

Driving again, lights flashing… some drizzle flecking the windshield. Mortie thought about the whole drug scene. He and Blackie knew some things about it. A lot of not very well connected things. Somehow he had to shake things up, to make them do something foolish. He knew one thing. Whoever was running the drug scene was pretty capable, pretty deadly, and pretty confident.

He had to shake that confidence just a little. He pulled up in front of a dusty sprawl bar in south Riverside. Over the entrance, red neon lights shaped like longhorns glowed against the night.

He sat for a moment in the parking lot of the Longhorn. Crushed beer cans littered the area in front of a chain link fence. He felt grey when he looked at this place. Death.... He was tired, suddenly. He did not like to decide things when he was tired. He should not go in there… he should leave. He went in. Bad country music was blaring. It was a big place. Some men and two women were at the bar. He went up to one of them, a well-built man in a cowboy hat. The man chewed on a toothpick. He did not seem surprised to see Mortie.

"Jablonsky, isn't it…?"

"Hello, Lt. Kline…?"

Kline smiled. Tight and hard. "That's me…." The sleeves of his shirt were rolled up, exposing a little UMC tattoo on a bicep. His hands were small and muscular. Compact. "A little out of your element, aren't you?"

"I like a little country music now and then."

The bartender came over. "A club soda…" said Mortie.

"What in it?"

"Just that…"

The bartender stared at him, shrugged, scooped some ice into a beer glass, and pulled a spigot, pouring soda into it. He tossed in a lime wedge and put it on the bar. Mortie reached for his wallet. The bartender shook his head.

"Soda is on the house."

"Weren't you working on a body in the park?" said Kline.

They stood without saying anything. Finally, Mortie said, "Going nowhere, fast…. We're reassigned to chop."

"I heard…" said Kline. "Welcome to the shit pile…" said Kline, and walked off.

Then there were just three men left. They were drinking and laughing and playing pool. One of them missed a shot… He threw his cue on the table.

"You want to play?" he said to Mortie.

"Not tonight," said Mortie.

"You don't like us?" said one of the others. They stood looking at him, holding pool cues."

"I'm sure you're a wonderful guy," said Mortie.

One of them tossed his cue on a table and sauntered up to Mortie. "A smart ass, huh."

"I am…" said Mortie, suddenly extremely tense.

He poked Mortie in the belly. "Kind of a marshmallow feller aren't you, Chubs?"

He reached toward Mortie. Mortie clamped onto the man's wrist, spun him around, and kicked him toward the pool tables. He reached in back of his shirt for his weapon. The door opened. Blackie walked in.

"Get your hand out of your shirt, asshole," Blackie said to one of the men. "And put down those pool cues…."

"Who the hell are you?"

A weapon appeared in Blackie's hand, pointed at the man. "The guy who's going to haul you in for threatening an officer, if you don't put down those cues. Or kill you…."

It was four in the morning. They were at a diner. "Would you have shot him?" said Mortie.

"I don't know…" said Blackie irritably. "Probably… What the hell were you doing down there?"

"Stirring up the dust. They've got to know we're around. How did you know I was there…?"

"You should have waited. I saw Kiriov…."

"How's the systems work going?"

"He wants me to move into that section," said Blackie. He took a bite and swallowed uncomfortably.

Mortie was strangely a little shocked. Somehow he felt dislocated, as though the earth had shifted just a little. "It would be a move up for you…" he said finally.

Blackie took another bite, and then put down his sandwich. He seemed suddenly sick.

"You okay, partner?"

"I'll be okay…."

"I'd hate to lose you as a partner," said Mortie. "But a promotion doesn't mean you couldn't work in the field with me."

Blackie sipped his coffee and grimaced. "I didn't become a cop to sit in an office. I don't think I'm capable of that, actually…."

Mortie described his meeting with Dickerson.

“God, I’m envious,” said Blackie. “What can I do to help?” He handed Mortie a printout. “It’s the profile we’ve built of all the communication links to date.”

“Who is in it?”

“Senevitch. Parks. I’ve been able to account for all of the calls coming in and out of Parks,” he said.

“Texas,” said Mortie, after scanning the list.

“Yes, and east… New England…” said Blackie.

“Plus, we got lucky with electric usage reports. Figerty over in accounting let me look through his files. There are some higher electric bills, but that’s about it. It’s pretty straight-forward stuff. There is a lot of turn-over in the parks… Floral usage… They buy a lot of stuff from Texas… and from some other places… But mostly Texas.”

“No obvious connections…?”

“No… But we’re still working on things.”

Mortie drove home. Exhausted.

One A.M. He ate a sandwich and drank a little wine and then slid gratefully between the cool sheets of his bed. The day buzzed around in his head. Numbers and faces. Mrs. Perlsworth … Thinking about her wasn’t going to get him to sleep.

Telephone numbers.

Faces.

He sat bolt upright. “Oh my god,” he said to himself.

He dialed a number. “Blackie?”

“What…?”

"Sorry to bother you.... Do you have that printout with you?"

"I was still up... Yes..."

"Good. Read me all of the last four digits of those telephone numbers."

Blackie read them. Toward the end... 4002.

"Stop... That number... Whose is it?"

"Don't know," said Blackie. "It's a city number. From somewhere in the burbs. It was one of the Senevitch numbers. We'll check it. We might need a search warrant. When did you see a match?"

"Today... And I have to check again to make sure of it," he lied.

"Who...?"

"I'd better be sure before I say, Blackie...."

"I'm your partner, Mortie," said Blackie, sounding hurt.

"Bear with me a few days...."

He lay back in bed. One of the numbers on the printout had the same last four digits as the one in Mrs. Perlsworth's book.

Fourteen

"You went where?" said Chief Powell, icily. Chief Powell looked as though some bad dream from the past… some nightmarish creature you think you have finally, totally, completely buried… had been uprooted and was wiggling around on his desk.

Mortie described his conversation with Dickerson.

Powell got up and began to walk to his window. He spun around. "Why, for god's sake? What got you to him?"

"A contact…."

"Who…? And why aren't you going through channels? Remember, Mortie? Your supervisor is Captain Groatly, the last I heard."

Mortie was silent. "Sir… Captain Groatly came in after… most of the main events took place. I'm just trying to understand something that began years ago."

"When…?"

"Before and after you came in…"

Powell flushed hotly "And what the hell bearing does this have on anything?"

"It bears on the victim in the park…" said Mortie. "And the victim had a connection with drugs… We think…"

"Mortie…" interrupted Chief Powell. "Do you realize how hard my job is?"

"Sir, I am aware that you…"

"I've got fifty constituencies. I have hundreds of officers. I have three divisions. I have twenty four departments. I have newspapers and TV, not to mention every rag who thinks they'll get notoriety by printing some wild rumor. And every one of them thinks they could do my job better than me." His face began to take on an unhealthy color. He pointed. A bad sign. "And you go down to some poor old retired guy and stir the pot? And you didn't ask permission before you went?"

"I didn't realize I had to ask," said Mortie, as calmly as he could. "You've got a tough job. Everyone says you've done a great job…."

"That's right," said Powell, heatedly.

"Dickerson says that after Blighe left and you took over, the informer network dried up."

Powell kicked a toe at a piece of expensive carpet. "I don't know that."

"The drug task force was dismantled."

"No choice…" said Powell. "I had a budget problem. Besides, Dickerson was ricocheting around like a madman. I know he was trying hard, but…"

"Didn't come up with anything?"

Powell shrugged. "Not enough to bother with."

"Why not…?"

"What do you mean, why not?"

"Was he given support…?"

Powell's face paled slightly. "He was supported…. And then there was the rake-off…"

"Did that really happen…?"

Powell leaned on the window sill. "I never thought so… Not really," he said, and sighed. "The opposition screamed for a supposedly independent investigation. It lasted ten months. It cost a lot. It was slow motion political torture. My enemies loved it. They were happy to keep it going."

"And…?"

"Inconclusive…" said Powell. "Perfect for them. They hauled good officers up in front of the committee. Three eventually took retirement and left. A lot of bitterness…."

"They didn't care about the officers?"

"They didn't care. They wanted to get me. I was new in the job. I had to sit there and take it. They strung it out…."

"Wow…."

"A freak show…" said Powell. He was silent again for a moment. "How was Dickerson?" he asked suddenly.

"He seemed fine. He asked about you…" lied Mortie. "Do you want me to stop?"

The light from the window caught Powell's face and body. Old… Paunchy…. "We worked together, you know," he said.

"I didn't know that."

Powell yanked a handkerchief from a pocket and blew his nose. He did not turn from the window. "On Patrol together.... He was a good man.... Mortie....?"

"Sir?"

"Mortie..." said Powell. "You're a rookie. You don't realize what these people will do. It's..."

"Sir..." interrupted Mortie. "With respect, sir. I'm not innocent. And I may be a rookie, but I can take care of myself. Plus, I have a great partner. So I'll ask once more: do you want me to stop this line of investigation?"

Powell turned. He was backlighted by the window. Mortie could not see his face. "What do you mean, 'stop'?"

"I mean, sir," said Mortie, "that's the other reason I didn't exactly go through channels. I don't want it to involve you. You're close to retirement... We could..."

Powell abruptly stopped him with a raised hand. The seconds ticked on and on. He sighed. "No..." he said at last. "No... Do your job...."

He came over and sat heavily in his plush chair.

"Mortie..." Blackie said from his desk the next morning. "Look at this."

"What is it...?"

"It's the video from Elm Street Apartments..."

Mortie slid his chair back and went over. "Anything...?"

"Not a lot...," said Blackie. "They keep the video for thirty days. It isn't the best, but it's better than nothing. I've been through two weeks of it. This is two days after

Senevitch died. I downloaded and scanned the whole time from the day before the death to yesterday."

"Already?"

"Yes," said Blackie. "They mailed it to me."

"And…?" said Mortie eagerly.

"Someone got to Senevitch before us…"

Blackie punched a button and ran the short clip. In the clip, a short, squatty woman is pushing a cleaning cart down a hallway. The cart weaves this way and that. She runs it into the wall, stops, looks around anxiously, jerks it back, and hurries it until it stops in front of 31b. She fiddles with something on the cart. She stands up. A man passes her. He stops for a moment, points down the hall, and gestures. She nods. She bends over and occupies herself with something on her cart. The woman is looking down the hall.

"She's waiting for him to leave…" said Blackie. "She's nervous. An amateur, I'd guess."

The woman dropped something, picked it up and looked up and down the hallway. Quickly, she opened the door and awkwardly jerked the cart into the apartment.

"So…? The cleaning service?"

"Except it isn't…"

"It isn't?"

"Nope… I checked with the manager…"

"Who is it…?"

"Don't know…" said Blackie. "She didn't know, either. It's none of their people. I've blown up the best shot I can get of her…." He held up a large, blurry photo of the woman. Mortie glanced at it. He looked again.

"Wait…" he said. "Run that clip again, will you…?" He looked back and forth from the blowup to the video. "She doesn't look like a professional. Look how nervous she is…. What is that she dropped?"

"Keys, I think."

"Run it again," said Mortie.

They ran it a dozen times more. Finally, Mortie shook his head and got up. "I know I've seen that woman before.

"Why, that's Mr. Andrews from 25b…" said the manager of the Elm Street Apartments a day later. "He's one of our retirees. A complainer," she said, pointing when they ran it again. "Always whine, whine, whining about something." She pointed at the video. "Look. He's at it again. A nice enough man, though. He always pays the rent at the last possible moment. What has he done…?"

"Oh nothing… nothing…" said Mortie. "He might be a witness, that's all…."

A tall, phlegmatic man answered the door of 25b. They explained why they were there. Mr. Andrews seemed unimpressed.

"Criminals…?" he said. "You can hardly get from the parking lot to your apartment without running into one of 'em…. If you want to know my opinion, it's the fault of those blacks and Mexicans. The way this county is going, no one is going to be safe. Until we get back to the country our Christian founders intended, we…"

"Elm Street Apartment seems a pretty low key place," interrupted Blackie mildly.

Andrews flushed angrily. "And that's just the kind of place they like to victimize, isn't it? Like that Senevitch fellow. Worked at a…, a *box* factory, I heard. You young guys. You haven't been around that much. You know what the problem with this country is?"

"Umm…?"

"Well, I'll tell you what… It's the fact that no one will get involved, that's what. Why I could be dying out there in the parking lot, and people would just step over my body. They'd leave me right there…! Just like they say on cable news. That's where the *real* news is. That man, Breckly, he tells it like it is. That's why the government is trying to suppress him. He says it's a moral problem. It's a *moral* problem, that's what it is. A moral problem."

"What's going on?" said a voice. It was a fat, fortyish man in a suit. He was breathing heavily and sweating.

Mortie flashed his badge. "I am Detective Jablonsky. We thought you could help us identify a woman. We…"

"Father, don't have to say a thing…!" said the man. His face began to turn a sweaty, reddish color. "You come here to harass an old man…? A retiree!"

Aghast, Mortie and Blackie stepped back, holding their hands out in stopping motions.

"No…. We…" they began in unison.

Several people stuck their heads out of their apartments, much in the manner of gophers popping out of holes.

"Call the police…!" yelled an old man in a falsetto voice. He lurched down the hallway, using the wall for support. "What's going on here?" he asked.

"No one is harassing anyone," said Mortie calmly. "Now, if you'd just lower your voice…."

"Listen…" said Andrews Jr., his face now an unhealthy wine color. He pointed a stubby finger at Mortie. "I'm an *attorney,* and I know what's going on. I've got a lot of friends downtown."

"Nothing is going on…" started Blackie. "We're just…"

Andrews Jr.'s lower lip began flapping. He began bubbling a stream of words and spit, as if steam might erupt from his ears at any moment. Mortie caught parts of it. "Abusing citizens…! Criminals…! A veteranwarhonestlawabiding…"

"Look," said Mortie, we're just…

"Just threatening honest citizens!" screamed the Andrews. "We'll sue!" bubbled first one of the two, then the other. The younger Andrews, whose facial color now made him look a sweaty, fat bulldog, lowered his head, and advanced toward them, sticking out first one arm, then another, like a scarecrow. It was something the whole family did, because he was followed by his father, who did the exact same thing… both of them screaming incoherently. Mortie and Blackie retreated a few steps and then leaned on the walls. The younger Andrews began pounding his palms on the wall. On one of his pounds, he hit the fire alarm. A loud ringing filled the hallway. Emergency lights at the ends of the hallway began flashing. Several doors slammed shut. People began streaming out of the building. The younger Andrews fell to the floor, ranting and kicking his feet like a child throwing a tantrum. An old woman poked at him with her cane.

"Move it, sonny. There's a fire or something."

The people walked around him. Andrews the elder sank to his knees, beseeching god, and screaming that his only son was dying. The people streamed like cattle toward the exits, ignoring them. Mort and Blackie leaned on the hallway wall. In a moment, Andrews Jr. stopped screaming, sat up, and looked around.

"You about finished?" he said.

There was a commotion behind them. Someone was rushing down the hall toward them.

"Who the heck is that?' said Mortie peering down there.

"I don't know. Wait! I think it's John and Missy…!" said Blackie

"Who…?"

"The TV reporters… They *are* everywhere…" said Blackie. "Where the heck did they hear about this?"

There was a bright light and a camera. "Yes, here we are again at the scene of a disturbance," said Droaning.

"That's right, John," said Missy, breaking in with huge, toothy, practiced enthusiasm. "On the scene of a violent demonstration, so you don't have to be. I think we recognize these two officers, don't you, John…?"

"Yes, Missy… Yes, it appears to be true." He pushed a microphone into Mortie's face. "It's our friends Officer Jabonsky and Blackman again, isn't it?"

"Jablonsky," said Mortie.

"What the heck are you doing here," said Blackie.

"Is it drugs again?" said Droaning, ignoring him. "Another killing? How sad a situation. An epidemic in our community."

"Look," said Mortie. "We can't talk about it in a hallway."

"There you have it, folks," said Missy smiling hugely. "The police aren't talking."

"They aren't denying that another victim has been found, either," said Droaning.

Missy pushed the camera toward Andrews Senior. "What is your role in this affair…?"

Andrews seemed stunned. "My role…?" he said. "Why, I've…"

"It's police brutality, that's what it is!" yelled Andrews Junior, who had stuck his ruddy, sweating head in front of the camera. "We intend to…"

"Come on, son," said Andrews Senior, glaring at Mortie. "Antiques Road Show is on, I think."

They slammed the door to the apartment.

Outside, Missy and Droaning had disappeared like smoke. A man was still there, apparently the boss. It was easy to see this since his phone rang incessantly and he almost never answered it. He would glance at the number on his Caller ID, and only occasionally would he flip open his phone, punch a button, and listen for a moment. Then he would mutter some inaudible thing and immediately hang up.

"Where did they go?" said Mortie to this man. "And what do you think you're doing?"

"What?" said the man. "People yelling. It's ongreat…! With the right support, it might go regional."

"Surely you're not serious."

"No, now that I think of it… probably not. You need tears, usually. When you get some emotion coming, you just keep that camera going until the crying starts. We fired a cameraman for missing some good crying."

"You fired him for being sensitive to someone's emotion?"

"No, of course not… *We're* sensitive… We *feel* for these people. We want to get them on the *air*. He just lost his focus… We can't have that now, can we?"

"I hardly know what to say…. But…"

"A death story is good," said the man, interrupting Mortie. "So long as the people don't have to look at a dead body. Our advertisers won't allow that."

"Your advertisers affect the news…?"

The man smiled the way one smiles at a child. "Well, of course," he said. "The news is like the cherries in the Jell-O. Family stories are good. Health is great too. Americans are the fattest people in the world, but they're fixated on health. You just throw anything in on health and it's golden." He held up a finger. "But…"

"But?"

The man cackled. "No fat butts…. The public is used to those kinds of things as real stories. You can feed them a story about a cat and they think it's news."

"Really…?" said Mortie.

"Sure… If Mrs. Jones' kitten is born with six toes, it's on the internet an hour later. Then we report it complete with a story about the incidents of five toeism, twenty minutes on the particular breed… You'd be surprised how many cat people are out there and interested. There's how you feed a cat, how cats are like people, videos of cats jumping fantastic distances, cats in the wild, feral cats, people who want to act like cats, the Broadway musical…. You could run some music… Great stuff! *Moonlight…! All alone in the moooonlight*," he warbled off key. "Oh Christ, yes, we could fill an hour with just cats. An hour… heck, a whole day…! There are whole channels devoted to cats. What am I saying? There are channels devoted to just Persian cats."

"It seems pretty boring…. Don't you try to inform the people?"

"Politics?" said the man. "Of course… Pundits insulting each other. Screaming is good. Or saying outrageous things about the President with a grin on their faces. Zingers… We call 'em zingers. Zingers! It's great. Almost as great as screaming couple stories."

"I've always wondered about that," said Mortie. "Don't a lot of them object to, you know, the intimate details of their lives played out in front of the world?"

The man stared at him as if he were the tenderest of innocents. "Oh no," he chuckled. "They *want* to be out there."

"I thought news was stuff like budgets of the cities or wars?"

The man's face assumed a startled look. "Are you nuts? You want us to show nineteen-year-olds coming back in those caskets? That won't work. Oh no… not by a mile…." The man's phone began ringing and ringing. He glanced at the number and ignored it. "We do put some serious stuff in; like school boards issues…"

"School boards are the real serious stuff?"

The man looked at him as if he were insane…. "Of course… The people go wild about their schools."

"Unless they're in a poor neighborhood…" said Mortie.

"Yes… Well…" said the man, in a voice that intimated he was starting to think Mortie wasn't his sort of person.

"Aside from being incredibly cynical, doesn't it get a little boring?" said Mortie. "And isn't the news supposed to be for the public good?"

The man nodded vigorously. "And you think that's the public good? We know what the public good is."

"What...?"

"When you end the news with a good, cheery sports story..." the man said. He saluted. "Ain't it beeutieeful...?"

They left. "We ought to have called the fire department..." Mortie said as they were driving. "Let them know it wasn't a real fire, so they don't send a big unit,"

"I did..."

"You did...?"

"While junior was pulling his tantrum," said Blackie. Text message. "Do you suppose they've done that before?"

"Oh... I would guess so," said Mortie. He turned onto Central Avenue.

"Quite the dog and pony show..." said Blackie.

"Quite..."

"Think they'll complain...?"

"Oh probably..." said Mortie.

"Think he's really a lawyer?"

"Hard to say. Maybe...."

"Think we'll be on the news?"

Mortie shrugged. "Haven't a clue...."

"Boy, we were slickern goose crap on that one, weren't we?" said Blackie after a few blocks. "Think we're in trouble again?"

"Oh, I would guess so..." said Mortie, turning onto Central again.

“Maybe we ought to back off for a while….”

“Maybe…. You think…?”

“Nah…” they said in unison, and they were laughing as they turned into the entrance to City Hall.

The rest of that afternoon and early evening they spent writing reports and doing paperwork. Later Mortie was driving home. He was turning a corner, listening to part of Stravinsky’s ‘Rites of Spring’ when suddenly he pulled over to the side of the road and stopped.

He knew where he had seen the cleaning woman.

“Amazing,” he muttered.

She was Finkel’s wife.

He was still parked there, thinking about it all, when his phone buzzed. “Mortie,” said Alice Birdwell. “Boss wants a word.”

“What time?”

“Mortie… You sound funny. Have you been up to something again?”

“That’s a laugh, Alice,” said Mortie. “We’ve been apparently sold to Parks like indentured servants. I’m dealing with a witch. There’s a body in the park that no one knows anything about, my union guy is apparently in league with the devil, and every department in the city, who, by the way, don’t seem to be doing anything else worth a sh…

“Mortie…!”

“…seem to guard their little pot of privilege like their lives depend on it. Your name is appropriate. It’s an Alice in

Wonderland re-run. I wouldn't be surprised if the Queen showed up and screamed 'Off with their head!' And you want to know if we're up to something?"

"So you've met Feldman?" said Alice.

"He met us," said Mortie. "Now we can't get rid of him."

"Don't talk so loud," hissed Alice.

"Why…?"

"Why?' she said. "Because he's the union guy. There's just one thing that can come from stirring up that guy. Trouble… Mortie…"

"What?"

"Why does Mrs. Welchly hate you?"

"What…? She doesn't… so far as I know," said Mortie. "I've known her through my mother all my life…. I mean I don't much care for her nephew Crogsly but…"

"Her nephew?"

"Now look, Alice. There's nothing to it, really. It's just one of those growing up things."

"Well, Mortie, welcome to the real world of competing interests. As for Mrs. Welchly hating you, I'm not surprised. People are very creative in their penchant for thinking up reasons to dislike one another. Get your tail in here in the morning at ten."

Fifteen

Across from City Hall was a vast glass-roofed atrium, containing shops too expensive for almost any human to even consider, as well as numerous eateries full of delicious calorie-laden food. Mortie stood behind a pillar, peering into this large, very public place as furtively as though he were following some desperate criminal, although to date, he hadn't followed a single desperate criminal, unless, of course, you include Downtown Brown, who was certainly a criminal, or at least had aspirations in that direction, though he wasn't often desperate. Mortie had agreed to meet his friend Birdy for lunch. Birdy, having no concern as to where he ate (the more public the better, he thought, for business) had picked the deli, a very public place.

The Atrium was an enormous place. Peering in the entrance and examining the surroundings carefully Mortie spotted a suitable table behind a large outgrowth of foliage, far to one end of the huge room and was carefully planning a route to the table.

"Mortie…?"

Mortie jumped as if he had been poked by a cattle prod. "Oh, hi, Birdy," he said. "I was just seeing if…."

"My god," said Birdy. "Are you hiding from the law or something? Oh, that's right, you *are* the law. Is this a stakeout?"

"No… I'm just making sure that someone isn't out and about …."

"Who…?"

"Damian…"

"The cook for the Tivoli restaurant? You're avoiding him…?"

"Yes I am…," said Mortie, peering intently. "Certainly… He thinks I'm his best buddy. He latches onto me like a wood tick. Hasn't that ever happened to you?"

"The last close friend I had was my dog," said Birdy. "For god's sake, a big strong cop, sneaking around to avoid a *cook*. Now I've seen everything," he added, plowing ahead, all the while making a great show of his entrance, talking with first this person, and then another, as he made his way to a table. He pointed grandly toward a small restaurant far across the atrium. "He's way over there, anyway…. You can stop crouching like that."

"The man has the eyes of an eagle," said Mortie, scuttling over behind Birdy to the table… although, Mortie attempting a scuttle, you must know, made him stand out like a fat man trying to do one of those traditional Irish dances where the arms are held still and the feet move. He reached the table and tried to line up Birdy with the restaurant across the large room. Feeling naked and with no small amount of desperation, he looked around for a waitress so that he could further conceal himself behind a menu..

"Mortie…! My Pisano…!" screamed a piercing voice from one of the kitchens far across the cavernous atrium. Dozens of heads turned to see who was making this unearthly noise, then turned to look up at Mortie and Birdy, apparently hoping one of them was famous. Seeing that neither was, they went back to their salads.

"What the heck is that?" said Birdy.

"Hello, Damian," Mortie said to a small, dark-haired man who had rushed over, embraced Mortie, and then plopped down into an empty chair.

"Ou arrr youuu my man?"

"Damian…" said Mortie. "As far as I know, you're Irish and your name is O'Doul. Why do you persist in this charade? Not to mention the fact that your accent is terrible…."

"My customers like eet…" said Damian, slouching apparently permanently into a chair and waving vigorously at someone across the way. "They are so stooped they don't know the deefernce. Eeet is good for le beeesnisss… They like eet when they think I am zee cook le famous. When I speaka de Francais, they think I am zee great cook."

Birdy pointed. "Don't you have to be in the kitchen…?"

"Eeet is noting," Damian said waving in the direction of his restaurant. "Sandwiches…, aaaah…, soup fram de stock… Everyday always the saam… Bah… Damian is a genius… an artist! He wants to cook, to create…!"

"Damian," said Birdy.

Damian waved grandly again, ignoring Birdy. "I hev l'assistaants. They all want to work with Damian. They take care of eet. All I do is give the orders… Sauce this… Plate that. They think these eees e cooking…Pah…. Eeeet is nothing… There is no *taste* today. This is not *taste*."

"Damian…" repeated Birdy.

"Eh…?"

"There's smoke coming out of your kitchen…"

Damian shrugged unconcernedly. He began turning in his chair… "Eeet is nothing…These grill restaurants there is always zee…" He paused as if unable to believe what he was seeing. A thin column of smoke was rising up, up, into the very top of the glass atrium. A grayish strato-cirrus had already formed high up. People were pointing. "Holy crap…!" he shrieked, jumping up and rushing off toward his restaurant ricocheting off startled patrons.

Mortie watched him go. "Think we should try another restaurant?"

"Oh… I don't think so…." said Birdy, examining the menu. "Let's order. If the food comes, we'll stay. If not, let's walk over to that street food kiosk on 4th; the one that sells those Coney Islands. Anyway, that ought to keep him for a while. Now what's good here today…?"

It was later. Smoke continued to emanate from Damian's restaurant. No one seemed to mind too much. Some firemen had showed up and had dramatically rushed in with tanks and hoses and several axes. There was a distant smashing and chopping noise and a sudden burst of steam. The people watched, chewing their food, and applauding, as though it were a stage show. The smoke stopped, and in a while the firemen came out.

But then Damian, who had not been allowed in his restaurant, went in and apparently saw what it had taken to quell the flames. He began dancing up and down and gesturing wildly. Some police showed up. One of them was gesturing emphatically to Damian. The firemen were implacable and began gathering up their gear.

Damian now began making huge chopping motions, somewhat like a referee in a baseball game calling a player out. The atrium was so large, and there were so many people inside, that watching the scene was like gazing at a distant scene across a chasm or canyon. There being absolutely nothing so focused as the lunch crowd, who, after all, are on a tight schedule, the other restaurants, their eyes on the hungry crowd, seemed intent on ignoring the commotion. The people alternated between watching the activity and stuffing food into their mouths.

"He should be in the theater," said Birdy.

Mortie ate his food… with relish. "People go to Las Vegas for this sort of thing. You should go over, maybe," he said. "Looks like some work there…."

"I was thinking, you," replied Birdy. "I'm waiting to see if Damian punches that fireman. You're the cop, after all…."

“No… These days I show up after the crime,” said Mortie, watching with interest, and taking another appreciative bite of his avocado and anchovy sandwich. “That would be a mistake on his part if he did,” he added.

“Well if he gets arrested, let me know. We have a criminal section,” said Birdy, getting up to go to the bathroom.

Eventually, the commotion died down. Someone in engineering had been summoned and managed to vent the smoke. Birdy left, but Mortie stayed a while to finish some paperwork. With most of the people gone and Damian occupied, it was a busy, but pleasant place. He was hunched over, trying to finish some forms, and was relaxing, finally, when he saw two vague shapes through the foliage.

Oh god, no…

It was Mrs. Welchly and Mrs. Higgenbottom.

“You don’t tell me…!” he heard Mrs. Welchly exclaim.

Mortie hunched down, trying to appear intensely interested in the ads in an auto circular he had found on a chair. “*89 GMC. High millage, good runner. BO.*” An image of Captain Blueheart popped into his head. *Blend, Blend….*

“Oh, I’m sure it will all work out,” said Mrs. Higgenbottom with a voice like a warm, wet cloth. She was a short, non-descript woman with a round face and brown sympathetic eyes. She wasn’t sympathetic, though. Not in the least – being almost totally devoid of that sort of emotion. But she looked like she was, and that was the important thing. She had the perfect face for her hobby, her occupation: Rumors…

Or rather, the pursuit of rumors. Mrs. Higgenbottom's one characteristic; her interest, her absorbing pleasure… no, her *obsession...* was the identification and collection of those butterflies of ephemeral information that floated through society. And not high society either. She wasn't picky. And not gossip, mind you, either. There is a difference between your average gossip, which is simply the repeating of fact, or half-fact, or no fact at all. Mrs. Higgenbottom was a seeker of truth. She was after the shining, gleaming thing; that tiny silver chalice that contained the wellspring, the source of it. She thought of herself as a free spirit on a vast beach in search of pretty shells. Only they were pretty shells only *she* knew about, for she had never told anyone of this need to look; this passion of hers. Was someone's daughter in a family way? No matter, she only knew them casually, or even second hand.

She did not know why she did this. She did not know why this set a hot feeling in her stomach and left her flushed with excitement, spent after a successful pursuit. Because that is what they were: pursuit. Through the years, she had begun to look upon these investigations as chasing a quarry. And she was not satisfied until she had run her rumor animal into its hole. Just say it, and she was off like a bloodhound, nose to the wind, or the ground… whatever it took, she would be off. And nothing would deter her. She wasn't embarrassed in the least to just ring a doorbell.

"Oh... Mary..." she would start, her mild eyes blinking a little in the daylight, as if actually shocked to see the person in question. "I was just here in the neighborhood and I had thought Mrs. Fetzweiller lived at this number." She would gesture meekly toward the street. "Well I'll just be off. I really didn't think there was that much chance of the Fetzweillers being here. It must be years since..."

"So it *was* true," she would say to herself on the way home. She usually had at least three going at any one time. Once something blew her way on the breeze of some overheard conversation, once she had heard of some alleged fact or comment, nothing could stop her from searching it out.

This was her life. She dreamt of it... She did not talk about this obsession. She did not tell anyone this. And she was thorough. A rumor wasn't collected until she had completely run it down to the hole it had come from. Once she had realized the satisfying, pulse-pounding effect these searches had on her, she had given herself up to this profession, for that is what she considered it to be.

And she never repeated these rumors, the shining light in her eyes visible to the world around her, was actually the gleam off of the pile of gems of information she guarded. Never had she talked to a soul about this.

Never.

Until she had become friends with Mrs. Welchly, that is.

Mrs. Welchly had deciphered this particular cant of mind very early in their friendship. She also loved rumor, gossip innuendo; really anything that could get her to where she wanted to go, or keep her up there on the pedestal. But she was of a more hard-bitten and practical mind, and was interested principally in the uses to which this talent could be devoted. And so, Mrs. Higgenbottom had become one of Mrs. Welchly's favorite protégés.

"Ah heaah," Mrs. Welchly would start, adopting her version of a southern accent she knew Mrs. Higgenbottom liked. "Ah heaah that the city is so broke they're plantin' half… ah say… half the flower of previous yeaahs…."

"Oh really," Mrs. Higgenbottom would say, flushing slightly, but feigning disinterest. She had no interest in the use of rumors, but one could almost see her nose begin twitching at such talk. One had merely to mention a whiff of a rumor.

Mortie resumed writing the report he had put off doing, glad to be partially hidden. The deli was quieting down. In the distance, he caught a glimpse of Gloria. Then he saw Caswell Crogsly. They walked off together.

"Wasn't that Gloria Aschenhault," asked Mrs. Welchly.

"It was…." confirmed Mrs. Higgenbottom.

"Mrs. Higgenbottom…!" Mrs. Welchly exclaimed. "I see that you know something…." She grabbed Mrs. Higgenbottom's shoulder and pulled her close. "Don't you *dare* keep it from me…."

"Oh…" said Mrs. Higgenbottom, flushing a violent, reddish hue of pleasure, "It's really not a final sort of thing. I wouldn't…"

"Oh fiddle-faddle, come now, you dear, you. Out with it!"

"Well… Don't quote me on this," said Mrs. Higgenbottom, almost whispering.

"What…? I can't wait!"

"They're getting married…."

"How *do* you do it?" exclaimed Mrs. Welchly, stopping in her tracks, for it was necessary to give Mrs. Higgenbottom her due. "That is gold! Really…? Married…?"

Mrs. Higgenbottom flushed with pleasure "Well… Not *yet*," said. "But I've heard they're engaged. He's going to give her a *big* diamond on the night of the P and F…." She was silent for a moment, as though reflecting on this event that actually she hadn't thought a thing about, other than the rumor, that is. "That Caswell's a pretty fast worker, I'd say…" she added.

"Well, well… they've known each other for quite a while…" said Mrs. Welchly breezily. "They grew up together."

"Still…" whispered Mrs. Higgenbottom, "It seems like more of a… how did we used to put it… an *arrangement*."

"Well, what do you expect?" said Mrs. Welchly, adjusting her hat to perfection. "People nowadays are so foolish. Marriage to you young people has to be so romantic."

Mrs. Higgenbottom, who was several years younger than Mrs. Welchly, accepted the indirect comment. She nodded. "I *think* I loved my husband.... It's hard to remember all the details." After a moment, she smiled weakly. "At least I said so."

"Well I knew what I thought of my Herbert," said Mrs. Welchly. "I was never expected to *love* Herbert. Oh, for heaven's sake, no," she laughed loudly at the thought. "I *liked* him well enough... of course... But love? Oh no, if I'd had to love him to marry him, we'd have never made it to the church on time, much less stayed together. Oh gosh!"

"Well, if you ask me, it's still a pretty sad way to do things," said Mrs. Higgenbottom.

Mrs. Welchly frowned down at her, but then nodded knowingly. "Oh fiddle-faddle...! She'll learn to love him if she knows what's good for her.... For heaven's sakes, they lost *their* money."

"All of it?" said Mrs. Higgenbottom in horror.

"Practically every last dime..."

"How bad?" said Mrs. Higgenbottom in a plaintive voice – for she was unerring in her proclivities.

"Bad..." said Mrs. Welchly. "I heard from Mrs. Roper that they've had to fire their accountant."

"Or he fired them..." said Mrs. Higgenbottom with an almost imperceptible chuckle. She then shook her head in guilty sorrow, for she thought of herself as an island of sympathy for the downtrodden and poor. "Probably not enough left to bother with. My god… Who do they…?"

"Not who," chuckled Mrs. Welchly. "It's *what*… They're using one of those *computer programs*…. Not enough to require an accountant."

Mrs. Higgenbottom shook her head at the thought of such a thing.

"Frankly, she should thank her stars he will take her," said Mrs. Welchly archly. "With that history, I think it's the genes. Yes, I think so, the genes are suspect." She raised a finger to make a point. "Breeding shows, you know… Breeding shows *every* time…"

"Well… he *did* marry a Catholic…" said Mrs. Higgenbottom. "Still…"

"Oh, I'm sure she will *like* him well enough," interrupted Mrs. Welchly. "Or, at least appreciate him after they're married. That is, if you believe in that sort of thing…. I hear she wants to go to medical school. I don't know, for the life of me, why anyone would want to do that when she can just have a nice home and enjoy life."

"And enjoy his money," chuckled Mrs. Higgenbottom faintly.

"Besides…" said Mrs. Welchly emphatically. "How in the world is she going to do that with no money? It doesn't grow on *trees*, you know."

"You don't need to tell me *that*," said Mrs. Higgenbottom.

"The *nice* thing… said Mrs. Welchly, smacking her lips with intense satisfaction as if she hadn't heard Mrs. Higgenbottom. "The *main* thing, is that she won't have to worry about money….

The two women walked a few steps further. They turned.

"Oh hello, Mortimer…!" said Mrs. Welchly crouching and pointing her finger, as if spotting him for the first time. "Hiding behind that pillar, were you? Some police thing, no doubt. Shame on you, you fox, you…."

Mortie walked across the street to City Hall, waved to the guards in the lobby, and headed to an obscure conference room two floors down from Chief Powell's office. They were sitting in an unused conference room on the lower level of city hall. Chief Powell and Captain Groatly were already there. Blackie came in and sat next to Mortie. A computer was open and operating on the conference room table. The Chief seemed very businesslike.

"Chief, d'boise here tinks they got a live one going…" said Captain Groatly.

The Chief nodded. "What sort of a live one…?"

Captain Groatly turned to Mortie. "Possible drug ring," said Mortie. "Shipping in the goods."

"What do you think, Captain?" asked the Chief.

"I tink dey's right. But I don't have a good feel for the whole thing."

“I agree,” said Mortie. “We aren’t sure of the parameters of this. But we think it is several layers, and we have evidence of drug packaging and distribution.

Chief Powell leaned forward. “How much evidence?”

“A witness and physical evidence of hard drugs.”

“How did you get this evidence?” asked the Chief.

Mortie thought that a curious question. “From a witness,” he said.

“Who?” said the Chief.

Mortie paused for a long moment. “From a woman named Perlsworth.”

“And who is she…?”

“A potential witness. She’s in the park a lot.”

“She’s a witch,” Blackie blurted eagerly.

Silence.

“A what…?” asked the Chief. He stopped them. “Wait… I don’t want to know…”

“It isn’t exactly her,” said Mortie, frowning at Blackie. “Someone she knows thinks she saw a drug transfer in progress. Why do you ask, sir?”

The door opened and Alice Birdwright came in with a man Mortie didn’t know.

Chief Powell held up a hand in a stop gesture to the others. “I’ve taken the liberty to ask Alice and Mr. Beavins from internal affairs.

Mortie suddenly had a sinking feeling in his stomach.

Captain Groatly frowned. “Sir… With respect, what does Beavins have to do with this….?”

The Chief stopped him and nodded to Alice, who cheerily plugged a CD into the computer. She punched a couple of buttons.

"Francine Flambou sent me this video…" said Alice. "Someone sent it to her. Probably they expected her to write something about it…."

On the screen, a video ran. Mortie gaped. Of course he had been on video before. But not like this. It was Mrs. Perlsworth and him at that coffee house. No amount of grainy video could suppress her allure. She was handing him the package. He saw himself looking at it and putting it in the bag. There was something horribly intrusive about it, something of the peeping through a window into a bedroom, though it was a perfectly public place.

"Is that her?" said the Chief.

"Yes," said Mortie. "That's us…"

Beavins stared at the video. "I'll say this for her, witches aren't what they used to be."

Mortie watched himself on the video, over and over, taking the package, looking at it and putting it into a bag. He began to have the insane notion that the figure might get up and walk away or turn into someone else. It didn't. It was just he and Mrs. Perlsworth.

"It's her," he said. "But it's nothing. She had called me. We had told her to call if she had any information. I had no idea what she had in mind. We were just meeting."

The Chief turned to Francine. "Are there any other copies of this…?" he asked.

"I don't know," she said. "Probably… If they want more, they're easy to make."

"Chief," said Mortie feeling a little desperate. "There's *nothing* to this… It was a perfectly normal interview. I wrote up a report that day and I turned the material in to the lab. Nothing out of the ordinary. I don't see the problem…."

The Chief rolled his eyes over to Beavins.

"We checked," said Beavins.

"And…?" the Chief said.

"Nothing…."

Fear in his belly. "The lab…?"

"Nothing…."

"I don't get it…" started Mortie, feeling for the first time in his short life that the moorings – those that held him steady – had come loose, and he was drifting. "We write our reports and put them in the file."

The Chief turned to Beavins.

"Tech's found nothing…" said Beavins.

"I don't think Mrs. Perlsworth would do it…" said Mortie.

"It isn't her, obviously…" interrupted Captain Groatly. "It's someone inside our office."

More eye-rolling toward Beavins. "Who?"

Beavins shrugged. "We're looking into it."

"Chances of finding out?"

"Depends…." said Beavins with a grimace.

"On what?"

"On how much you want a scandal."

The Chief blanched. “We have to think about this.”

Captain Groatly looked at Mortie. “Unless you didn’t file a report.”

Funny, Mortie noticed that Captain Groatly seemed to have lost his colorful Ward Six inflections. There was a long silence in the room. The video played over and over. Mortie wished he could reach over and stop it, but knew that would be a terrible mistake.

“What is the point of this video?” said the Chief to Alice.

Mortie… A flash of Dickerson... *You don’t have to shoot someone to kill them off.*

Her eyes were calm and blue. “That’s easy. It’s a gun aimed at you and the Mayor. That’s the point,” she said. She pointed at Mortie. “Through him…. They figure to get it out and into the media. The election is coming up.”

The Chief groaned.

“Uh… Captain…” said Blackie, who had been fidgeting around with his small laptop and had placed it on the table.

“I think…” started Captain Groatly.

“Captain…?” repeated Blackie.

“Yes Blackie…?” said the Chief.

Blackie considered them with pale, icy cold, calm eyes. “All of this is impossible….”

Everyone stared at him.

“Why…?” said Groatly.

“Because,” said Blackie, “in the first place, even if something is erased, it is still in the computer…. The person who did this stuff must be pretty stupid. I have a copy of that meeting on an external drive. We have copies of the notes on that meeting."

Everyone in the room was staring at him. He had plugged in the computer and was scrolling down through a file. "We…" he nodded toward Mortie. "With the Captain's okay, we operate a little differently than the other detectives…. Once a week, we type up the notes of each day's significant doings. Anything of importance goes into them."

"You keep copies of public files? That's an…"

"They're encrypted," said Blackie. "And always left at the station."

"He's right," said Captain Groatly, leaning forward. "I forgot about that. I thought dis was a good ider at the time… Detective Blackman is very good wit dese machines. In fact, I been usin' him for some systems analysis…."

Captain Groatly's jocular speaking pattern had somehow returned.

"It wasn't my idea," said Blackie. He tilted his head. "It was Mortie's. It's a pain, but we do it anyway. Ah… Here it is… Mortie's notes…." He spun the computer around toward the Chief.

Alice scanned through the notes. She nodded to the Chief. A palpable sense of relief flowed back into the room. Something in Mortie unclenched. The Chief turned to Alice again. Relief fought with anger in his face. His lips had a peculiar whitish hue. He rapped the table suddenly with his knuckles.

"What next...?"

"We have to tell the Mayor," said Alice. "We probably can run this down, but if something comes up, it's up to us to make sure he isn't blindsided."

"Tell him," said the Chief. "Write me a short report on the whole thing. Let me know what he thinks." He turned to Alice. "Thank you for coming." When she and Beavins were gone, he turned back to the others. "You expect more shipments, is that it?"

Mortie nodded.

The Chief turned to Captain Groatly. "I want you to push it..." he said, angry now. "Push this goddamn thing all the way...."

"Legal..."

"The usual," said Captain Groatly. "We'll get the goods from the Court in order to do the surveillance. "We want whoever they are to think they've moved us off of things."

Mortie didn't know what was going on. Was he off the case? Or worse?"

The meeting was breaking up. Mortie got up. His legs felt shaky. He realized he had been tensing his whole body.

"A word with you," said Chief Powell to Mortie. The others left. They sat in silence for a long moment. Finally... "I don't have to tell you how easy it is to get in trouble over this sort of thing, do I...?" said the Chief.

"No sir...."

"I think we ought to let you go…."

Mortie felt as if his body weighed a thousand pounds. He could not speak.

"We'll let it be known you and Blackie aren't working the case. You and Blackie will set up a command center, not at the office. We'll reimburse you and supply what help you need. You'll be monitored by Legal. But by somebody I trust. Can you do that?"

Relief flowed back into his body. "Yes sir, we can," he said.

Back in business.

Outside City Hall, Mortie stopped and took a deep breath. He felt like a man who'd walked to the edge of some cliff in the dark. He had the sudden but absolute realization that he would never take anything for granted in police work again.

His phone rang.

It was Mrs. Welchly.

"Mortimer," she said gaily. "How are you, dear? I was wondering. You know how well I think of you and how I'd wished we could continue our little talk the other night."

He took a deep breath. "Hello Mrs. Welchly. Yes, it's too bad we didn't get a chance to talk. Everybody's really busy right now. With what…? Oh it's boring stuff. Certainly I will get to you as soon as I get a break. I'll get together with you shortly, you can be sure of that. You can count on it for sure. Goodbye Mrs. Welchly."

Evening. Mortie was exhausted. He had a salad and a sandwich. After a while, he poured a double shot of Bourbon over some crushed ice and sipped it, sitting on his small deck.

In a while, the phone rang. "Mortimer..." said a husky female after the fourth ring. "You cad. You promised to call. We aren't pleased...."

"Francine...?"

"Well it ain't Mother Teresa, dearie. Who'd you think it was?"

"I've been really busy..."

"That's what they all say... You owe me for that CD business. Now give me something hot and juicy and I'll forgive you."

"Zippos, Francine. As in, not too much. There's been a lot of auto theft east, and we're working on that. It's a big problem. Not very exciting work, though."

"So what happened to the deceased?"

"Which deceased?"

"Which deceased? The dead guy in the verdant field by the rippling waters, that's who! The guy, name of Senevitch, found in that glade in the park where heretofore only juvenile passions were released – that's which deceased..."

"We've run down most of the leads... We're off of it for the time being. It's still an open case. What do you know about Kiriov?"

A pause. "The book store guy?"

"Yes...."

"Gets around at night. Lots of rumors about him. Deals in this and that... Always at arm's length, of course.... Doesn't do dope, as far as I know. Books, of course. Not much else..."

"A guy named Jackson..."

"Never heard of him..."

"William Packard..."

"Nope... What's all this about, Mortie...?"

"Mrs. Perlsworth...?"

"I knew it! That woman Perlsworth! You were seen with Mrs. Perlsworth...!"

"How in the heck did you know that, Francine...? Anyway it was strictly business," Mortie said.

Francine screamed a laugh. Mortie winced. "Strictly bidness, says the big cop; wink, wink, nudge, know what I mean? Know what I mean?"

"This isn't Monty Python, Francine..."

She cackled again. "I don't care what kind of business it is. The way I heard it, she's someone to change spots for... Mortie?"

"Yes..."

"Speaking of such things. What's up with Gloria Aschenhault...?"

"What about her?"

"Well I always thought you guys were going to be the main thing...."

"I think she's occupied with Crogsly these days," said Mortie. "Look, Francine. This is all…."

"Oooh… The eternal verities. Hit a nerve there, didn't Francine? See you, Lieutenant Mortimer. Jablonsky…."

Sixteen

If Mortimer Jablonsky had one redeeming talent, other than his hands and arms, which were naturally powerful, it was his ability to get information simply by talking to people. He was large, but so unthreatening and relaxed that people said things they wondered about afterward.

"What could those two stoners possibly teach us," said an exasperated Blackie, who preferred technical means to getting that same information.

"There they are," said Mortie, pointing out Jesus and Burt, who were lounging on the corner of a miscellany of junky payday loan stores, taco stands, and vacate buildings. "We have to get the word out that we're working chop," he said. "If we talk to enough people, the word will get around…."

"How does the chop-shop business *work*?" repeated Jesus, with a look of amusement mixed with contempt at the question's utter stupidity. He looked around uneasily. "Look," he said. "We're legit now. We've got a business.

And it doesn't help to be seen talking to you guys. No offense intended."

"None taken," said Mortie mildly. "What's your business?"

"We got a tow truck," Burt said proudly. "We built it ourselves…"

"Hey, yeah," said Jesus, pointing out a derelict duel wheeled Chevrolet truck, sturdily, but haphazardly equipped with a hoist. "Burt here learned to make these wrecks go like wicked crazy up in the hills where he's from."

Blackie was frowning at Burt. "Where's that?" he said, still of the opinion that they should have run those two in for possession of marijuana.

"North Carolina…. I was raised twenty miles from where Jimmy J. was born…." said Burt.

"'Jimmy', who?" said Blackie.

Burt was scornful of anyone who didn't know that. "The great Jimmy Johnson, that's who," said Burt indignantly. "The greatest stock car racer in history. Ever'body up there grew up around cars; runnin' 'em, fixen' 'em, tearing 'em apart, the whole thing. Ever'body did that stuff natural as picken sang. Had to. Most people didn't have no money they hadn't spent. We could swap out an engine before you could look twice."

"Stay legit, "said Mortie. "And if I ever get to where I can help, somebody might get you a contract. But that's not what we're interested in."

"What…?" said Jesus, peering down the street. "This, … like, ain't doing our image too much good."

"Just like I said," repeated Mortie. "How does the chop-shop business work?"

"In the first place, it's big," said Jesus. "None of this is any secret, by the way. You got your cruisers, and break-in wiring artists, your drivers, you got your break-down guys, your mechanics, and your dump guys. The cruisers spend a lot of time cruising, usually parking lots. Shopping centers are good. College parking lots are great. Just get a class schedule and you know where the students are going to be. They drive nice cars these days, too. Anywhere where the chump has to go in for a while."

"How long does it take to…?" started Mortie.

"A minute or two," interrupted Blackie.

"They drive it away… like a stolen car…?" asked Mortie.

"Amateurs…," said Jesus scornfully. "Usually they run the car up onto a flat-top tow rig and the car is hauled to a shop, where it's broken down."

"What are they interested in? Motors…? That sort of thing?"

"Anything sellable…" said Jesus. "They break down the car, engines, engine parts, starters, any high-performance stuff, seats… Whatever is in demand, they get.

"Seats?"

"Sure, if they're any good," said Jesus. "Like I say, anything. The engines are parted out sometimes. That way, they can't be traced as well. If things get a little hot in one city, they accumulate a semi load and haul it to somewhere else."

"Isn't that a violation of interstate commerce laws?" said Mortie.

The light in Jesus's eyes grew brighter. "Oh, I'm sure…. They're terrified at some commerce guys… Besides mostly they sell locally. Junkyards are in on it, though they don't like to admit it. Usually, it's a junkyard where the stuff looks like normal…."

"They don't seem too afraid of police."

"Nah…. Insurance companies pay. By the time the part numbers are traced, they're long gone."

"Why don't the insurance companies publicize the losses…?"

"Because," said Jesus. "They've figured out there's no percentage in shouting out about auto theft. It's not good for their business. It's easier to just jack up the rates in the areas where it's high. Hey, everybody benefits; the car-jacker, the junk guys, even the lawyers… particularly the lawyers. They dress the guy up, talk nice to the DA who's usually overloaded with serious crimes, force a jury trial, and settle. Most guys get short sentences and are out – if they get any time at all."

"What stops it…?" said Mortie.

"Lock bars, publicity, GPS trackers…" said Jesus. He frowned. "Automatic sentences for the guys caught… Now can we get out of here…?"

"I came in after most of it happened," said Captain Groatly.

They were standing in a brightly lit alcove in a hallway. Groatly had almost the same *did-you-have-to-bring-this-up* look as Powell had had when Mortie described his meeting with Dickerson.

"He actually talked wit' youse…?"

"Yes… Briefly…."

"How? Why…?"

"Was Dickerson out of control after Chief Powell came in?" Mortie said after a moment.

Groatly shook his head. "He was a good officer," said Groatly. "So I wouldn't say that."

"And yet he left?"

"He left of his own accord," said Groatly. "It was his choice to retire…."

"You were here when Blessing died…"

Groatly flushed. "I was. What's the point?"

"What happened…?"

"What does this have to do with anything?"

"To be honest, I'm not sure," said Mortie. "But we think the current drug scene was set up by those events. And we think the same people are running the hard drug operations. There was an investigation after Blessing?"

"The report is around here somewhere. I can get you a copy…" said Groatly. "When I took over, we moved to calm things down. To make sure that everyone was doing dese tings by the book."

Groatly scowled at his phone.

"What's with your phone?"

"The damned thing doesn't work…!" Groatly said.

"What happened?"

"I don't know. I was just trying to put the buzzer thing on and it locked!"

"Let's see it…" Mortie said.

Groatly thrust the phone toward him.

"Oh… You locked it…" said Mortie. "Let's see, your number is…?"

Groatly told him. He punched a few buttons and then showed Captain Groatly how to unlock it. "There… All fixed…" he said.

Groatly took the phone looking at Mortie as if he were some new species of human. "That's amazing…."

Mortie said nothing. It was about as amazing as turning a light switch on or off, which he realized *had* been once amazing. In 1900….

Groatly thrust the phone back into his pocket. He shifted oddly on the balls of his shoes. He made a jerky and vague gesture. "Um… Mortie…"

"Captain…?"

"Maybe you should go up and talk to Overbight about this ting…"

"Can I do that?" said Mortie.

"Sure," said Captain Groatly. "He ain't dyin' of cancer. He's just dryin' out…"

A copy of the report on the Blessing death was on his desk when he returned from a break.

TacCom Report #03- 42A report concerning the events of July 14, 2003.

Mortie opened it and began reading the dry report. *On said evening, officer Blessing approached…*

Blessing had not gone easy. A desperate brawling fight. A mess... A bloody sickening mess. Broken glass… Tables... Hair and skin under fingernails… Blessing dead. Two others. Diagrams… Car locations… Forensics… Blood spatters… Bruising… Knuckles… Hair…

Brain matter…

The rest of the report. Telephone communications before and after. Three dead. Blessing dead… Dead… Dead… Overbight's testimony… Overbight's testimony… Overbight's testimony. Overbight….

Oh god… He felt dirty. He went to a water fountain, ran the water until it was cold and tried to wash the sour taste from his mouth.

Seventeen

Mortie waited for Overbight on a sunny patio overlooking a lake, watching wind riffles sweep across a blue lake. He tried to think of something to say. The drive north had wound through an impressionist's dream of dark green pastures fringed with pastel trees and verdant pastures. Young corn waved in black fields by a little river. He had loafed along, daydreaming a little. He was happy to be in the country. Warm air came gusting through an opened window, smelling of freshly cultivated earth and of an early cutting of alfalfa and… a pig farm. It had seemed like such a fine, generous idea coming up here, when Groatly had said it. Now he was sure it wasn't. He loved the drive, but the further he went, the less he wanted to actually get there – to intrude on someone's life. He felt more than vaguely embarrassed, as though he had fallen into Groatly's suggestion without thinking. He began wondering if he had been gullible… again. He drove and drove and thought about this. And although he tried to think of a reason for these feelings -- so that he could exorcise them from his head – he could not name it, and that seemed to make it worse.

Overbight was a small, pale man, slighter than when Mortie had known him, he thought. But maybe that was from being at this place. He was mostly bald. He looked like a down-and-out store clerk.

Some Mallard ducks began gabbling loudly again – chasing each other around and making splooshing noises.

Mortie stuck out his hand. Overbight shook it. An icy, hard grip. They sat. Overbight eyed Mortie and said nothing. He lit a cigarette.

"So, what can I do for you?"

"Thanks for meeting with me."

Overbight spit a bit of tobacco. "It's a little boring here. I get a smoke break, so…"

"How's it going?

"It's going…." Overbight shrugged. "It never ends with the sauce… So what's the deal?"

"You were working chop-shop."

"Yes," said Overbight. A wariness in his eyes.

"We've been at it for about a week."

Overbight nodded. "I heard you were working on a body in the park."

"Yes…" Mortie nodded. "It's unresolved."

Overbight laughed. "Unresolved…. You young guys…. No leads…." He looked off at the lake.

"There are leads."

"You still partnering with Blackman?"

Mortie nodded. “Sure. We need anything you’ve got on the target area. It seems a big problem that nobody seems to think is a problem. You’re a veteran and you know that area. We’re rookies. It’s as simple as that.... I...”

“Look,” said Overbight grinding out his cigarette. “I don’t know why you came up here. But let me tell you this... Chop-shop is where they send you when you’re a rookie. They figure you’ll blunder around and not be too much trouble. Most of the people in that section are poor, or at least not as rich as the rest. So they send you there. You show the flag, make a big to-do; that sort of thing. You arrest a few guys. Not much harm done. When you leave, everything goes back to normal.”

The ducks on the lake rose in a rush, set their wings suddenly, and settled a hundred yards later.

Overbight lit up another cigarette, sucked hungrily on it, and shifted in his seat. “Or when you’re like me, over the hill and useless...” He looked straight at Mortie. “And you’ve killed your partner...” He was silent for a while.”

“You didn’t kill your partner,” said Mortie quietly. “And I don’t think you’re useless. Fifteen years isn’t it?”

“Yes, fifteen big ones,” Overbight said, his voice breaking into a strange cackle. He shifted around uncomfortably in the wire chair. “When I was a kid, I dreamed of being a hero. I really made a big difference, didn’t I...?”

“Iverson... He...”

Overbight scowled. “What about him...?”

"Doesn't seem to want us in Parks…"

Overbight was silent for a moment. "I don't know. There was some scuttlebutt about his partner…"

"Kline…?"

Mortie had a sudden impulse to talk, checked it, thought about it, and then on the spot decided to go ahead.

"Chop-shop is a blind for us," he said. "We're still working the park…."

Overbight nodded. "It seemed odd. So chop is a cover…?"

"It is…. And we could use any help you could give us."

"We were workin' a drug case when Frank got shot…. It was a muddy deal. We really didn't know that much, or we would have been a lot more careful. I was supposed to be there. I was late. I thought it… we both did… that it was going to be an easy deal; just a stop to do some jawing. You know, the type of thing you do all the time."

"I read the report…."

Overbight stared at him. "I had a couple of drinks. It was supposed to be no sweat. Jablonsky, there ain't no easy deals, and heroes are guys who make the least mistakes." His eyes glistened. He seemed to shrink inside his clothes. "He's dead, anyway."

"You were saying something about Kline…"

Overbight waved it off. "Nah… Forget that… Just talk… Look. We fish in a river of shit. It's easy to get smelly in our occupation. You just do the best you can for as long as you can. If you're around long enough, two things are going to happen. First you're going to make people mad if you do your job right. And secondly, you're going to make mistakes. You just hope you don't have to pay too much for the privilege. Talk is cheap."

He pointed vehemently at his chest. "I know. They sure as hell talked about it… Even some of the guys I worked with. I saw the way they looked at me. They didn't have to say anything. Somebody was raking off the drug bust takes. Newspapers couldn't get enough of it."

"Did you ever consider those newspaper stories might have been plants?"

Overbight considered him. "No…." He started to light another cigarette, but dropped it, tried to pick it up, and dropped it again. "Ah… shit," he muttered. He looked away and then at his watch. "Well, I've got to get back to the fight." He sat for a moment. "There's a list of contacts I built up," he said. "It might help you a little. Really, you've got to get your own contact list because most of these things are personal, you know. Ask Captain Groatly to get it out of my desk. It might help…."

Mortie got up. "Thank you, sir…. For what it's worth, when you're ready to come back, we'd be happy to work with you…"

Overbight stood up; shook his hand. He started into the building and stopped. "Jablonsky," he said. "I thought you were some kind of rich screw-off. I might have been wrong." He paused. "Watch out for Iverson's partner…"

Mortie stopped. "Kline…?"

"Kline..."

Overbight was gone. Mortie could see a reflection of a blue sky in the glass door. The highway spooled up in front of him and away in the rear view mirror.

Overbight....

Defeat....

Despair....

Blessing....

Somebody smart had come in....

You don't have to shoot someone to kill them off.

He wheeled through some green hills. Black asphalt wound down, down a long hill. In a way, it's better. Worse for them, better for you. They're still in their jobs. Just can't do much. You just make them part of you. You just pump some sewage into their reputation. Clever. They become dead. Useless. The walking dead.

He opened the windows and turned up the radio to try to wash the feeling out of his head. He stopped at a roadside stand and bought some sweet corn and tomatoes. He shoved a CD into the player. Maria Callas... and then some head-banging rock. Nothing.... He finally turned it off and listened to the ziiiiiiiiiiiiiiiiiiiiii sound of the asphalt under his tires. In the city, someone honked and he got stuck in some traffic, and this was somehow comforting.

Home. Mortie put on Chopin's *Waltz in C Sharp* and puttered around. Evening. He cleaned up a mess in his kitchen and made a large salad. He poured a glass of wine.

His phone buzzed. "It's Melissa…"

"Mrs. Perlsworth?"

"We should meet…."

They were sitting on a bench in a park. Melissa glowed. Gorgeous.

"So what can I…?"

She kissed him. A wild, long, fiery kiss. His hand brushed her breasts. She moaned. She held his face with cool fingernails and ran her fingernails down his neck. "My big teddy bear. I… I'm sorry," she said huskily. "I know we should be more…"

"My god!" said Mortie. "I loved it…"

He kissed her again… And again…

"Friday night…" she said.

"What…?"

"Oh nothing. It's just something we do…. Kind of a ceremony…. We get together at the rock…"

"Yes?'

"We have a candlelight march down to the river…."

"And?"

"Well… I was just thinking… You could pick me up when it's over. We could go somewhere…"

"Go somewhere…?"

"And play a little…. I've been thinking of it. You want to, don't you?"

"Yes…" blurted Mortie.

She smiled. "You'll do anything I want, won't you, teddy bear?" She ran a fingernail down over his face and smiled mischievously. "Will you do as you're told, Lieutenant?"

"Yes," he croaked. "What time…?"

She told him."I have to go," she said.

He did not remember the drive home.

The road back around to Finkel's office was still a fine collection of bone-jarring, hard, clay holes. Finkel was sitting in the middle of a small ocean of paperwork, talking on his phone. The clock was still ticking. At Mortie's entrance, his thin face lit up, and then as quickly dimed to a doleful, but determined focus on his work. He waved Mortie toward a seat.

"No, I meant Delphiniums… Del… phi… ni… ums…. Yes – five hundred. Yes, yes, yes… okay…." The remains of his ponytail had come loose. Wisps of grayish brown hair stuck out.

"Thought I'd give you an update on the victim in the park…" Mortie said, looking around. "You're busy…"

Finkel peered at an old computer screen. He nodded. "Hang on a minute… Flower Festival…. Three weeks…. We've been extremely busy."

"Still…? A lot still coming?"

"Yes, quite a bit," said Finkel glancing at his screen. "As you know, the Flower Festival is a very big thing. People come from everywhere to see it."

"Expensive…"

Finkel nodded. “It’s gotten out of control. But when people do come, they want to see a show. They don’t want to see nothing. And those people spend money in town.”

“I’ve heard. It’s a big economic jolt to the city….”

“Bigger than most people think. We expect at least five thousand visitors just for the show. But it’s an ongoing thing, too. Aside from the perennials, which we’ve got to encourage, we plant about five thousand annuals, plus the annuals planted by seed.

“You grow your own?”

“Some of it…” said Finkel. “We have several grow houses. We’re fortunate to have good help. Ortiz runs the grow shops…. We plant several thousand tulip bulbs in the fall. It takes a lot of sweat and teamwork to get it all delivered so that it is in the ground in time to look good.”

“How long should they be in the ground…?”

“Oh, depends upon the plantings and the weather. Several weeks to six weeks…. So, we have deliveries coming every week now… It’s as much an art as a science.”

“Look…” said Mortie. “I wanted to let you know that we’re pulling back on the investigation temporarily. We’ve got a lot of work to do also. Plus we’re shorthanded.”

Finkel looked up. “And…?”

“So we’re wrapping up our work on the body and the park work in general. There are just a couple of items I’d like to run by you.”

Finkel nodded and kept making notes in a ledger. He seemed very old and tired… “Shoot,” he said.

"Speaking of which, Senevitch, the dead guy drowned. He wasn't shot… Or rather, the bullet didn't kill him."

Finkel looked up with a quizzical expression. Nothing else. He shrugged. "So what do you make of it…?"

"I don't yet… I do have a theory or two…"

"And?"

"And I'd rather not say just yet…" said Mortie. He took out a very grainy enhanced reproduction of the video photo they had retrieved from the Elm Street apartments, and which Blackie had enhanced. He shoved it across the scratched and worn desk.

"Do you recognize her…?"

Finkel stared at the photo. He held the photo up so that the light caught it. He seemed to shrink. He looked up. A ledger in his hand crinkled. An ineffable sadness passed across his face like a cloud shadow… and then was gone.

His face became expressionless. He looked up. "No…" he said. "I can't say that I do… Is it a woman?"

"It *is* a lousy photo," laughed Mortie, getting up. "Well, if you hear of anything, you know where to find me."

Finkel had spread the wrinkled spreadsheet out on his desk and was sorting around through the rest of the paperwork as Mortie left.

Eighteen

"I need a real estate agent," said Mortie to his mother.

"Wonderful!" she exclaimed. Then she frowned a little. "But don't you think you ought to wait to buy a house?"

"It isn't for that. It's for… something else. It's nothing, really, and it's for a short time."

"My friend Hilda is a real estate agent…."

"Hilda Nightingale? Doesn't she sell those high-buck homes? I don't think she's for us…."

"Well, yes, million dollar and up places. That's true…. But she might know someone…."

Hilda Nightingale's office occupied a considerable portion of a Georgian Mansion high up on a hill in a forest on the southwest end of the city. Mortie sat several yards away from Hilda, on one side of the vast gleaming expanse of her gorgeous antique desk. It was made of the sort of mahogany that might have come over on the Mayflower, were it not slightly larger than the Mayflower, an antique that could have only been constructed when the world was young, the empire intact, and no one doubted that's the way it ought to be. The huge desk was in the middle of an even huger room with wraparound windows and many flowers outside, with birds twittering at Hilda's request. Though it was merely nine in the morning, Hilda was made up in a costume that included a huge, bright red hat.

"All the world's a stage," she told the women who worked for her. "Dress the part." She had fired agents who came to work un-made up. She considered Mortie from across the expanse of her desk. "You want what, darling?"

Mortie explained the sort of place he needed.

"So… Downtown and downtrodden…?"

"That's about it."

Hilda grimaced, a startling sight. "Dare I ask why…?"

"I'd rather not say…."

She considered him for a moment. "Well… Okay… For dear Constance, I'll see what I can do."

"Can you show us something now. We're in a bit of a hurry. And not too Expensive, I hope…."

"You dear, silly man, you," laughed Hilda…. "How you talk! *I* won't be showing you anything…." She laughed again at so funny a joke.

"But?"

Hilda picked up her phone and after a long moment, Mortie faintly heard a gravelly voice say hello. "Mumford…" said Hilda. "Do you still have…" She saw that Mortie was listening, smiled broadly, and punched a button on a machine, producing a comforting shussching sound, thereby also drowning any overhearing. "Thank you…. That's fine…" she said when he could hear her again. She put down the phone. "Mumford just might be able to help…" she said briskly. "He's in business down there…."

"Mumford?" said Mortie, the beginnings of alarm in his voice. "'Mumford' who? You don't mean Mumford the Mole, do you…?

"It's Mumford Molaire, and that is an unfortunately applied sobriquet," Hilda said coldly. "A fine person when you get to know him…." said Hilda.

"He's in real estate?"

"In a manner of speaking…"

Mortie vaguely recalled some conversation with a relative. "He went to *jail*, didn't he?"

Hilda laughed, a laugh that managed to be warm and cold at the same time. "Oh that…" she said, gathering some papers and sliding them out of sight. "But a nothing. A misunderstanding…" she waved grandly. "A small thing…. He's out now. He has a little operation down on 7th and Central… That southwest corner…. He does little jobs for me now and then. Recalcitrant renters, and all of that…. We try to keep him busy. He tends to get somewhat destructive when he's bored…."

"I've heard," said Mortie, trying to recall that corner…. "Hasn't that corner been condemned…?"

"Oh god, no…!" she frowned. "How dare you say that…! Well, maybe. Anyway, Mumford has a pizza business there…. You can have the whole upper floor. There's even a bathroom…. Besides…" She stood up abruptly and fixed him with a baleful stare…. "Beggers can't be choosers. Now can we?"

A few days later… Mortie left his apartment and made his way through traffic toward downtown. Once he turned onto a street and parked, watching the traffic pass. After a few more blocks, he parked, and entered a nondescript building a few blocks from downtown. On the second floor, he knocked at a door. In a moment, Blackie opened it. The room had a long table with four computer monitors. In one corner, piled haphazardly, was a collection of electronic equipment. Three people occupied the computers, none of whom could grow a beard. One of them was fat and unshaven. Another was thin with an acne problem. This child was staring at a screen also, and sucking on a giant sized Mountain Dew. He wore dirty jeans, a t-shirt, and a baseball cap that read *Cubs 03*. He looked as if he were in junior high school.

"Fortleman has to leave…" said the fat one staring at the computer. "We've just about got it, anyway. He has school in the morning…."

"Which college…?" asked Mortie.

"High school," said Fortleman. "Writes algorithms on the spot…. Very useful in dealing with the data…"

"What's he doing here?" said Mortie, alarmed somehow at the sight of Beavins from internal affairs looking over one of the computer operator's shoulders.

"That's it…" Beavins was saying. "Okay, go back… Okay… Okay…"

"We've got to have him," said Blackie.

Mortie looked around the dingy space. "Not much of a place…."

"Perfect for this," said Blakie who loved it. "We couldn't risk being found out. All of these guys are volunteers. And there's pizza close by…."

A man Mortie didn't know was tapping at a laptop. "That's Skilling from Legal…" said Blackie. "He volunteered to run interference with the courts."

"What have we got?"

Nineteen

One of the things that is interesting about John Blackman (I think you all know this), was that he operated at a speed roughly twice what a normal person would. But two things slowed Blackie down. The first was night. He loved the night – the later the better – but more to the point and somewhat oddly, he seemed to operate better, to think better and more surely, in the dark of the night. He did not know why this was. The other thing that calmed him was rain, or more specifically, the sound of rain on a car roof. Rain on the roof in the dark of the night was like some strong narcotic to him.

And on this night there was both. He had been sitting for thirty minutes in his car with the rain drumming and thrumming on the roof of his squad. For a while, he had turned on his computer and had done some work, but the glaring light of the computer bothered him, and so he had given up, and turned it off. He sat in the dark, watching the bouncing of thousands of little bright prismatic spouts lit only by the white cone from a distant street light. He watched and listened with a calm, intense pleasure. For it really *was* raining, steadily, insistently. Every so often, it would slack a little, and then he would think, with a slight pang of loss, that it was going to stop…. But then it would start again, harder this time. The drumming had slacked again, and then continued in a steady roar, pouring continuously for the last hour. And it was a dark, inky dark, black night.

A car pulled up next to him, the lights dancing through the sheets of rain on the asphalt. Out of this inky, wet dark, Mortie rushed from his car, flinging himself into the front seat of Blackie's car. Mortie did not care for rain, at least the sort that got him wet. With a good book by a fire, crackling lightning outside, he was fine.

"Man," he said, futilely brushing the rain off his clothes. They sat in Blackie's unmarked squad car, not saying a thing as the rain drummed on the roof.

"We're about ready?" said Mortie after a while.

"Yes," said Blackie. "We've been through every phone record, every bank record, and all criminal histories of every person we can find who has worked at the park. We have taken all of the material of Dickerson, Overbight, and Senevitch, and analyzed each against all of the others, going back as many years as we could. We've tracked all of the calls to and from the number you found on Senevitch's match book. We assembled all of the old numbers and names from the old files of Dickerson and Overbight."

"Lots of work…."

"I had help. We got really lucky, Mortie."

"We did? How so…?"

“Senevitch’s apartment had been tossed pretty good. But they missed something. Aside from those matchbooks, that is.”

“What?”

“A cell phone. Senevitch apparently changed phones sometime before he died.”

“So?”

“So he left the old one in a box in the closet.”

“Wow… exclaimed Mortie. “You mean he just left it?”

“Yes… Lots of people do that. I think I have three…. Somewhere….”

“Are the numbers still good…?”

“It doesn’t really matter,” said Blackie. “From any number, even old ones, we can get information, credit cards, banking, and addresses. I assembled a team from IT. In the end, we had hundreds of numbers and names. George Macon – you remember him with the neural networks?

“Yes… Don’t understand it… But a nice guy.”

“He created an algorithm for us to help cross match names, dates, and progressions. He coordinated with the telephone company. The search warrant allowed us to search all of the records, public and private, for the individuals associated with this case. We’ve attached photos to as many of the numbers as we could. In addition, we’ve acquired DNA samples from as many of the people of interest as possible.

“And…?”

"We're still looking through it all. Information is still coming in…

"Communication…."

"We're going to be on secure links when and if this thing goes down… We should have it all in a day or so…"

"And…?"

Blackie passed him a one inch thick printout. "The cover sheet is the summary."

Mortie clicked an overhead light, looked at them, and scanned through a list of numbers. "About what we thought…."

"Yes… Someone named William Packard."

"He's the main guy…?"

"It looks that way…" said Blackie.

"What's he look like?"

Blackie handed him a picture. A fifty-year-old man leaned on a doorway, smiling vaguely at a young woman with a clipboard. A nothing of a man. Completely forgettable

"His real name is John William Buford. We think…. He's got a criminal record going back thirty years. New Jersey and LA, mostly. Not a thing since the 90's."

"He got smart," said Mortie.

"A very careful person. He buys those cheap phones you can buy anywhere. He thought that would shield him. But we were able to get an address for him…"

"And…?"

"It's a townhouse. It's three townhouses."

"Three? He owns three townhomes…"

"Rents…. He's got three separate addresses paid by a corporation. Pays for all of them. Managed by a local company. NPM. Nationwide Property Management."

"Did we get their…"

"We did not. It might have alerted him and it wasn't necessary…. We'll get them when this thing goes down. They have no reason to think there's anything below board. They love it. He pays on time every time. He's cagy. He uses a different one for each trip. They don't know. They think he's a salesman. He's not flamboyant, but he's very popular in every place. He sponsors little league teams. Very quietly though. No picture, no publicity. Makes donations. He has an annual barbecue in one place. They think he's great."

"Pays on time," said Mortie. "No muss, no fuss. We got that picture?"

"Yes…. We sent someone up to knock on his door. Got it from across the street. He stood in the doorway. Acted casual but he wouldn't come out. The picture is pretty good, considering. He's very cautious."

"DNA?"

"We tailed him. He smokes. We got a water glass, too. Several samples. They're being analyzed."

"Do we have everything in place…?"

Blackie listened to the rhythmic drumming of the rain on the roof for a moment. "Pretty much..." he said. "We can't get phone records for all of the workers. Most of them don't have phones.."

"Who doesn't have a cell phone these days…?" asked Mortie with mild shock.

Blackie shrugged. "They usually get those phones you buy time on when they need them. We're still assembling things.

"Do we know where…?" asked Mortie.

"No…. We have tails on the main players…."

"Good guys?"

"The best we've got…. I think it will be Friday night…."

Blackie frowned. "The night of the P and F, for god's sake? Why do you say that?"

"I don't know. I just think so…" said Mortie weakly, the taste of Melissa Perlsworth, and the feel of her lips, and the smell of her in his brain…. "So, it's all set, then. We just have to watch until it happens."

They sat in silence for a long while. The rain was slacking now. The descending coda of the sound of rain left Blackie with a vague, but palpable feeling of loss.

"Yes…. We've done about what we can do. It's up to them now."

Morning …. Three days until the Police and Fireman's Ball.

Mortie was gasping.... His legs hurt. His arms ached. His eyeballs felt funny. Sweat poured off of him.

"Up...!" Abby Roedes yelled.

Everyone struggled to their feet.

"Right...!" Abby Roedes yelled, diving to her right. A selected group of her slaves were supposed to follow her every motion. They had been at it for twenty minutes. She dove to the right and rolled onto her back. "Up..." she jumped to her feet. She dove to the left and rolled. "Up!"

On and on and on. "Stop..." she gasped. "Okay, great. Rest. Breathe...!"

It was later.

Fourth Street and Carriage. "I only just thought about it," said Mortie.

"You're kidding..." said Blackie.

"Why shouldn't I take her to the dance?" said Mortie, a little miffed. "I thought you'd be all for it. I need a date. She's beautiful and..."

"She's old enough to be your mother," said Blackie.

"She's nothing but gorgeous."

Blackie shrugged. "I guess...." He shook his head at Mortie. "Just about the time I've got you figured, you come up with this..."

"But I decided not to..." interrupted Mortie.

"Why...?!" exclaimed Blackie. "You just said you were going to take her..."

"You know why. Because she's a part of this investigation, if only a peripheral part. When this is over, then maybe. I just..."

"Who are you going with, then?" asked Blackie.

Mortie coughed and read the number on a phone call that was coming in. "Well... Vivian called me...." Mortie muttered. "Wait, I've got to take this...."

"Who...?" said Blackie after Mortie hung up.

"Oh, no one you know," said Mortie blandly." His voice became almost inaudible. "Her name is... ah... 'Vivian'."

"Vivian Chart?" exclaimed Blackie. "You mean, Vivian the Shark?"

"You know her?"

"Everyone *knows h*er," Blackie said, turning to him in mock astonishment. "No one likes her. I *thought* you didn't like her..."

"I don't..." said Mortie, in a conspiratorial voice. "And she can't stand me, either. See, that's the beauty of it. No commitments.... Complete lack of any complications. We just go and then we...."

Mortie's phone sounded again. He looked at the number. "Oops, I've got to take this...."

"Mortimer?"

"Oh hello, Mother.."

"Are you busy...?"

"Kind of...."

"I just wanted to tell you that I'm not selling the farm."

"Well... that's good..."

"I'm giving it to you…"

A silence. "Ma… I can't afford that farm…"

"Oh, don't worry," said Mrs. Jablonsky. "It won't happen right away. You'll have time."

"What was that about," asked Blackie after he had hung up.

Mortie shook his head. "Apparently I'm going to be landed gentry…."

"The farm…?"

Mortie nodded.

"Wow…. You'll be rich…. That's great…! You won't have to be a cop."

"Great…" said Mortie.

Twenty

The Coordinating Committee meeting of the Police and Fireman's Charity Ball was held once a month until the weeks before the night of the soiree, when it was held once a week. It was a complicated affair and Mrs. Welchly was intensely busy, ruling over four committees and the myriad of details which made up the plans for the ball. This, the second to the last meeting before the actual event, went on late into the evening.

"And let me be clear," she was saying with a frown. "We must have the orchestra there as early as five o'clock. No later…."

"They're musicians…" someone was saying to her. "They stay up late. They don't like starting that early…."

"I don't care what they like…" she said. "They'll just have to get used to it this once. If they don't like it, they'll go elsewhere for work."

She looked up. Alice Birdwright was in front of her.

"Mrs. Welchly," she said. "Could I have a few minutes with you…?" She motioned toward a room. Mrs. Welchly stared at her. "I don't think I have time right now…." she said "I'm busy…."

"I'm sorry. I have to insist…"

Mrs. Welchly laughed harshly. "*You* have to insist? That's a hoot."

"Look…" said Alice. "It's either that, or be interviewed at the police station…"

Mrs. Welchly rose to her full impressive height. "You think that you can threaten me?"

Alice shrugged. "Okay… No matter…. I'll report to the Chief…." She began to walk away.

"Wait," said Mrs. Welchly. She turned to some others who were attempting not to listen. "I'll be back shortly," she said. "There's an empty room this way." She led the way into a vacant alcove.

Twenty minutes later, Alice Birdwright came out. Mrs. Welchly came out a few minutes later.

"Now, where were we?" she said to the others.

Alice got out of the cab two blocks from the Chief's home. She walked slowly to a small park. The Chief was sitting on a bench by a pond, tossing bread to some very quarrelsome ducks. She walked up and sat down. He tossed more bread. Their bills made little snapping noises.

"Look at that one…" he said pointing.

"Which one?"

He tossed a crumb to the ducks. One of the ducks, horribly fat, barged through the water with amazing speed to get to the crumb, rudely shouldering the others aside.

"That one… You talk to her…?"

"I did…."

"Well....?"

"She didn't like it."

"Big surprise.... Was it her that got it...? The video...?"

"Yes.... She denied it, but yes. Not directly though...."

"How did she do it?"

"She has allies.... There are people who don't like you, and they want the mayor out."

The Chief tossed another piece to one of the smaller ducks, who watched dumbly as the fat one barged in and grabbed it.

"Who?"

"Well Iverson and his partner Kline, for starters. The word is that Kline is involved in some shady deals."

"I know...."

"You know...?"

"Yes...."

"Why don't you just get rid of him? You're the Chief."

"It's not that easy. You know that.... Kline and Iverson are tied in with a lot of people, some of them with influence."

"I know that, but..."

"Hopefully, we've got something going now to put a hitch into this whole drug scene. With a little luck..."

"What....?"

"Alice..." said the Chief raising a hand. "We'd better stop. I wouldn't want you to have to lie in court. She talked to Kline?"

“Apparently she met him,” said Alice. “But after that, the main one who talked to him was her nephew.”

“Who’s that?”

“A young man named Crogsly…”

The Chief looked at her. “Who?”

“A nephew.”

“So she is doing all this for her nephew…?”

“She hates Constance Jablonsky who won’t give her the time of day. Frankly, I don’t think Mrs. Jablonsky knows she exists.”

“I think I’m getting this,” said the Chief. “She hates Connie Jablonsky so she goes for Mortie. She figures she can get at me and the mayor with that and still keep her distance.”

Alice nodded. “That’s the way it seems.”

Chief Powell was silent for a while. He tossed a piece of bread far to the right. The fat duck barged over there and the Chief tossed the rest of the bread to the others. “Well then, okay…. She’s out of it….”

Alice sighed. “No… That’s not the way it is, and you know it, sir.”

“What…?”

“You can’t leave anyone standing….”

Powell had been leaning forward, his elbows on his knees. He sat up and looked irritably at her. “What the hell are you talking about…?”

She shrugged. “You know what I’m talking about. If you merely wound them, they’ll do it again. Mrs. Welchly isn’t innocent and she isn't easily put off. She has allies and she'll get more. She hates the Jablonskys and there are lots of people who don't like you and hate the mayor. The next time they'll be more successful. And they won't be as merciful as you. You've got to get them totally out of the game."

They sat for a while in silence. "I'll think about it."

"Sir, you pay me to tell you the truth, right…?"

He winced. "That's right, I do…. And I have a feeling I'm going to get another dose of it."

"You have to either do what's necessary or…"

"Or what…?"

"Or get out…." she said.

Powell did not respond to this. "We have to let the mayor know about this…."

"Me…?"

"Naturally…. Let me know what he says. No paper. So, what are you going to do?" he said.

The ducks milled around, their beady eyes glaring at them.

"When…?" she said.

Powell shrugged. "When I'm out of it… After this is over…."

She pursed her lips and leaned back. "I don't know. Something will come up."

"What do you make of my nephew…?" he said.

"Smarter than people think," she said. "Thinks broadly, but slowly. Not mean enough. That might get him killed off. Too young right now. Potential for bigger things."

Chief Powell leaned back on the bench. "Keep an eye on him for me, will you…?"

"I'm not sure he wants to be looked after," she said. "Or that he'd take my advice, anyway. He's pretty headstrong." She was silent for a moment. "I'll do what I can." She was silent again. She shifted around uneasily. "I've got to go," she said.

"Huh…?"

"I've got to go…."

"Yes, I suppose this is boring…."

"No," she said, getting up. "All of those ducks splashing around makes me have to pee."

Twenty One

It was a perfect late spring night. An enormous yellow golden moon rose in splendor on the eastern horizon, hung there for a while as if to allow people to admire it, and then ascended further, changing to a silver orb. At the Riverside Country Club, the air was warm and filled with the wafting scent of lilacs – of a quarter mile of fresh, purple bloom. The orchestra began hooting and tooting their warm up notes. In the morning, the whole place had been aired out, turned out, and polished to a high gleam. Trucks came and went with a small mountain of produce, and now all of the other scents mingled with a delicious smell of barbecue and expectation.

That same silver moon was now casting a pale, white light on all, including the unmarked car Mortie and Blackie were sitting in.

Earlier than that, a phone had buzzed.

"He's moving!" Blackie had said in a low, intense voice. They had followed slowly, and slowly they had moved in…

They were watching now, through light-enhancing binoculars, toward a collection of old warehouses six blocks south of the park.

Early in the evening, at twilight Mortie and a plainclothes officer watched a parking lot. He pointed out a car. "Okay, Bob," he said. "That's her car. When she moves, follow. And call. And let me know where she's going."

They were anxiously watching the buildings.

"Is everyone in place?"

"Yes," said Blackie. "We've had him covered for days now…."

"Hard…."

"It can't last. He's too good not to pick it up after a while…."

"The phones?"

"Encrypted…."

Mortie's phone buzzed. "Yes… Okay…" he said. "She's coming this way…."

"A car is coming. A sedan."

He stared into the night. His back ached. He suddenly realized he had to go take a leak. "Okay…" he said. "Wait, now… Everybody sit tight."

"Can you see them?"

"Yes… It's… Four… I can't see… One's a woman…" said someone. "I think."

The four got out of the cars and moved quickly between the buildings. Some figures got out and quickly entered one of them.

"Now…? Should we move…?"

"Wait, everyone…?" said Mortie over the radio. "No talk… Move on my go… "Okay… Go…" he said after a moment. "Move quietly…." Mortie sprinted toward the building. The windows were covered. But through one of the windows, he caught a glimpse of a woman.

Mrs. Perlsworth, laughing and gesturing.

Mrs. Perlsworth, stacking packages.

Mrs. Perlsworth, cupping a man's face and smiling.

"Slowly now," muttered Mortie. "Move in slowly and we'll bag the whole…"

"Who's that?" said Blackie, pointing at a white truck. The truck rolled slowly to a stop. People got out and began setting up. A light came on.

"Goddamn it, it's Missy and John…."

A squad car roared into the clearing, siren suddenly shrieking, lights flashing. The lights in the building went out. Sound of glass smashing. People running. Falling. Cursing.

"Who is that…?"

"Go! Go!" yelled a voice.

"Stop…. Police!" screamed a voice.

"It's Iverson…!"

"What the hell?" yelled Blackie.

Mortie saw a figure jump into a dark sedan and disappear out to the north, between a building and some sheds on the fairground.

"Go after that one. That's him!" A light winked, and then the report of a pistol. More blasts.

"They're shooting!" someone yelled.

The fleeing sedan sideswiped a building and accelerated toward a newly built enclosure. Boards flew everywhere as the sedan hit the fence, bounced onto a street, smoked rubber, and fishtailed away.

A small figure stood in the middle of the street, directly in the path of the fleeing sedan, his hands at his side. The white cone of light cast him in an odd white halo. He raised his left hand in a ridiculously calm 'stop' gesture, as if he were directing traffic at a picnic. When the sedan did not stop, the man raised a weapon. "Pop… pop… paaang, pap." Steady firing. Shots from the sedan… metallic ricochet sounds. The small figure's weapon winked, once, twice, three times. The figure did not crouch or move. Mortie heard none of those shots. A confused barrage of firing. The figure jerked like a rag doll, twisting to the street, rolled, and then tried to stand up, but sagged back as if dragged down by some great weight. The figure fell to his side.

"Who the hell…?" yelled Blackie as they raced on past.

"Overbight…" Mortie yelled. "Keep on that car!" he yelled.

"*Code six…!*" Someone yelled. "Officer down. Fairground. Any squad… Block entrances on 6th! Stop any car coming out of the fairground…!"

"Heading for Ballroom Drive," said someone.

The sedan swerved around an oncoming car through a hedge. A person rolled out of the car as it skidded around a tight corner.

"I'll get him," yelled Blackie, and was out of the car. Mortie jammed the accelerator down.

"He's trapped on Ballroom Road!" Mortie yelled into his radio.

Mortie rammed the rear of the car to try to get it to stop. A light winked at him from the car. *Shooting at me*, he thought. Faster and faster. Lights ahead. Patrol cars… The car swerved wildly, jumped a curve, and turned right. The car flew through the circle in front of the Ballroom, ran over two small trees, and raced across a large flower garden, past twenty or thirty gaping couples in formal dress.

Chief Powell, the Mayor, Mrs. Welchly, and Caswell were standing together in front of a small crowd next to the pool.

"Mayor… our City Manager, Selectmen," Mrs. Welchly began. "I see Senator… On behalf of the Police and Fireman's organizing committee, I take the greatest of pleasures," she started maintaining her severe smile.

There was a loud crash and a dark sedan ricocheted off of a fire hydrant rocketed forward, slid sideways, and plunged into the newly cleaned swimming pool while sixty people gaped. Any number of off duty officers fumbled for their weapons.

One individual who was in sight was Caswell Crogsly who was talking with Mrs. Welchly by the pool. He was showing her a ring and waiting for Gloria to come out. At the commotion, they turned. The car plunged into the pool. A wave of water drenched them.

"My god…!" said Crogsly, as water ran off of him. "The ring!" he screamed as the diamond and platinum flung upward, performed an arc, and made a tiny plunk on the deep end of the pool. Flinging water left and right, he dashed over there and jumped into the pool. After much flailing around, he came up coughing.

Captain Blueheart looked down at Crogsly floundering in the pool. "I say, Crogsly," he said. "You'll have to put on more sail to make headway in there. Did you find it?"

"The drain," said Crogsly, as someone poked a pole at him and pulled him onto the edge of the pool… "I think it went in there…"

"Well, they can always drain the pool and look," said Captain Blueheart. "It might turn up…."

Mrs. Welchly stood as still as a statue, the smile still implanted on her face. The destroyed hydrant was now a fountain that was shooting fifteen or twenty feet into the air. A small river was flowing away toward the big river. A mist came down on everyone including Mrs. Welchly. She took out a silk handkerchief. When she moved, a small stream of water ran off the rim of her hat and down her bosom. "Well," she said, carefully dabbing at her face. "I'm glad they just cleaned the pool…."

Mortie stopped his car and jumped out, his weapon drawn. The whole crowd gaped.

"Hands up!" he yelled as a figure emerged from the car in the pool.

A man brought Mrs. Welchly a beach towel. After holding it out to no response, he began vigorously toweling her off.

"Get away from me, you pervert," she hissed, jerking the towel away from the man. "Go tell them to bring my car up." She stared at Mortie with intense disdain. "I might have figured that man had something to do with this," she said. Turning, she strode toward the entrance, leaving a dripping trail of slightly chlorinated water, the people blankly staring at her and parting like the biblical sea. But before she had traveled half the distance of the ball room, she met Mrs. Jalonsky and her escort the Lt. Governor of the state, both of whom had stepped aside like the rest of the astonished crowd.

"Mrs. Welchly!" said Mrs. Jablonsky. "Do you need any help? My car is outside. I'd be happy to let you…"

"No thank you," said Mrs. Welchly with a frozen smile. "Take a good look, Constance," she muttered, as she walked out of the entrance. "Because if it's the last thing I do on this earth I will see that you and your offspring regret this." She shook herself and got into her car.

The orchestra, oblivious to what had happened, struck up Hoagie Carmichael.

"Beside the garden wall," someone sang.

The man who exited the semi-drowned car held his hands over his head. Now there were a half dozen members of police force with their guns drawn. Several holstered their weapons and yanked the man out of the pool onto his belly.

"Is anyone left in the car?" a cop yelled at the prone man.

Alice had moved up behind Chief Powell, who had produced a weapon and was holding it pointed at the moon. "Get in there and check you fool," she hissed. She gave him a shove.

Later, the Chief insisted that no one pushed him, that he had jumped into the pool of his own volition. Fortunately, it was the shallow end and he was able to wade over and peer into the car. The mayor, no fool, jumped in beside him. Ascertaining that no one was home, they turned in time to have their pictures taken, the Chief with his pistol still pointed toward the moon. The Mayor looked resolute.

"It felt like D-day," he said later, though on D-day he'd been in the catering corp. in Britain.

It was over. Others were seeing to the car in the pool and the arrested man. Blackie came along.

"How'd you do," Mortie asked.

"Haven't gotten him yet."

Flashes flashed. Mortie shielded his eyes. Two or three reporters began talking at the same time. "How does it feel to be a hero?" one yelled. "We heard you shot it out with them."

Mortie smiled weakly. "I'm no hero…"

"It's the best thing!" exclaimed one of the reporters. "What a story!"

It was later. Mortie and Blackie had gone to see to all of the men who had helped on the bust and write brief summaries of the action.

"We've got another of them..."

"The woman...?" Mortie asked.

"Not yet."

Mortie sighed. An image of Mrs. Perlsworth flooded into his mind. "Too bad."

"Yeah," said Blackie. "Mortie. Too bad."

It was twelve thirty before he changed his pants and stopped at the hospital. He thought about going home. Vivian! His date. He went back to the ball. He had been exhilarated. Now he felt like an empty gas tank.

Gloria was dancing with Captain Blueheart and talking animatedly. He looked around for Vivian, but did not see her. He stood at the bar watching the people sweep around the dance floor. People cast furtive glances at him. Some pointed.

Then Gloria was standing by him, beautiful in a blue evening gown. "Well Mortie," she said. "I'll give this to you, you sure know how to make a mess."

He nodded.

"Your date left," she said.

"I guess...." Mortie smiled ruefully at her. "What happened to yours?"

"He got all wet.... Then he got all mad."

"Mad...?"

"Oh... something about a ring. Went to change his clothes...."

"Too bad..."

She waved. "No... It's all right. I was never that impressed with money anyway. Vivian is perfect for him. So what do heroes do when the battle's over?"

Mortie shrugged. "Overbight once told me that heroes are the ones who make the least mistakes. Go home, I guess."

She nodded toward the orchestra. "Look, Mortie, this dress is gorgeous, if I do say so. There's an orchestra, a dance floor and a big fat bright moon. Seems a shame to waste it. Want to dance a couple?"

Mortie suddenly felt better. He held out his arm. She took it. The orchestra struck up G... L... O... R... I... A......!

"My god!" Captain Blueheart said, poking a bony elbow into his neighbor.

"Eh...?" said the man. What do you want, Blueheart? Not more of your damned boats and the like?"

"No by gad!" said Captain Blueheart, pointing as Mortie and Gloria took the floor. "Look... What a couple they make, eh...?"

And then the band was playing more Hoagie Carmichael and it finally did turn out to be a really good party.

They were parked at an overlook by the river eating lunch.

"We didn't do much did we?" said Mortie.

"Not really...," said Blackie. "But we stopped it and maybe gave some comfort to a couple of old guys."

"And we got Packard…"

"Where…?"

"Stopped on the freeway… It was a matter of time, anyway…. He knew it…. His lawyer met them at the station."

"And…?"

"He's not talking…."

"Surprise, surprise…."

"Yes…."

"Did we get his property management firm NPM…?"

"Yes…. They're assessing it now…."

Mortie felt completely empty. The end of this, such as it was, didn't feel anything like he had expected. He had expected to be exhilarated. But nothing. A letdown. Depressing.

"Overbight dead. God what a mess," he said.

"He went out the way he wanted….," said Blackie. "There's going to be a big funeral. And a memorial for his partner Blessing. He lived long enough to know he had been set up and that we had broken them. For now…

A car came bouncing down the rough road and stopped by the river. A little man got out, went around and opened the back. He struggled to lift out a large object.

"That's Finkel, isn't it?"

"Ummm," said Mortie.

"Want me to stop him?"

"No," said Mortie. "I don't think so…"

"It's a clock!" said Blackie. "What the heck is he doing?"

"Watch…"

Finkel hoisted the clock onto his shoulder and walked to the river. "Sploosh!" went the clock. He picked up a long pole and pushed the rapidly sinking clock out into the current.

They got out and walked down. If Finkel saw or heard them coming he did not acknowledge them. He watched the clock float away and sinking. It disappeared in a swirl of brown current.

"No more clock," said Mortie.

Finkel looked up. He seemed younger; almost unrecognizably so. "No… No more clock. I won't live my life that way anymore…"

"Your wife was involved with the marijuana, wasn't she…?"

Finkel looked at him, but said nothing at first. "She knows nothing about anything," he said. "But you know, sometimes a person's priorities get … misplaced."

"What are you going to do?"

Finkel smiled grimly. “I’ve done it. I quit. We’re leaving this place…”

“Well,” said Mortie. “Let us know where you’re going…”

Finkel laughed. “I will…”

Night again…. They were sitting in Blackie’s sedan. “Look at this,” said Blackie, snapping on a light and shaking a newspaper at him.

“Mayor and Police Chief in on Bust,” screamed the headline. A long story by Francine ensued.

“So Mrs. Perlsworth wasn’t the real witch….?” asked Blackie.

Mortie snapped off the light. “No… The real leader of the coven is a housewife from the south side of town. She came forward after it was over.”

“What was she like…?” said Blackie.

Some traffic flowed by in front of them.

A drab little brown sparrow of a woman had approached Mortie; a woman with an absolutely opaque expression. She was carrying a shiny purse. It was the only shiny thing about her.

“I’m her,” the woman said.

“Who…?”

“The witch… I’m her…”

“Mrs. Perlsworth…?” asked Mortie.

“Came to some of our gathering… She was never the leader.”

“Why are you…?”

"I just wanted it clear," she said. "We're not like her… And we don't like publicity; at least that sort of publicity."

The tiny woman had left.

"What was the real leader like?" said Blackie.

"Not like Mrs. Perlsworth," said Mortie after a pause. "We haven't picked her up?"

"No," said Blackie, who glanced at him and smirked. "She left a note you know…"

"I heard…"

"It says she was at the warehouse because you wanted her there…."

Mortie shook his head…. "We haven't found her?"

"No…. *Who* is Mrs. Perlsworth?"

Another, even longer pause. "I don't know…" said Mortie. "I don't think we're done with her."

Blacke smiled a little. "You mean you're not done with her. I hear Iverson is out."

"It seems so," said Mortie. "Early retirement."

"His partner Kline?"

"Nothing so far… I'd like to have caught him."

"Maybe still… There's some sort of an investigation going on."

"Senevitch…?" said Mortie.

"Was making cardboard pots with false bottoms in his spare time."

Blackie fiddled with his radio. "We're guessing they looked him up at first. It was an easy jump of logic. They were working with park stuff and they looked up who made those cardboard pots. Senevitch wasn't making much at the box factory. He took a little money from them at first. And once he found out what they were doing he was trapped. He couldn't get out of it. Before that he'd used a few drugs. He started to use more."

"So they killed him...?"

"No. They didn't trust him, but they didn't kill him. They kept an eye on him while their deals were in the works. They needed him. Or at least they didn't want to dispose of him yet. But then he took to fooling around by the river. He drowned. It may have been a heart condition. I don't think he cared any more. They were going to get rid of him anyway... They were keeping an eye on him. He drowned. They hauled him to the tree and..."

"Why?" asked Mortie

"They weren't interested in Marijuana..." said Blackie. "Too small a margin, I guess. But they didn't want it going on with their deal going so they thought the body would keep us busy. We're just guessing, but they figured it was quite a clever thing. They knew someone was dealing marijuana out of the park."

They were quiet for a moment.

"But what I still don't understand is why shoot him?" said Blackie. "Why not just leave it alone. If they'd done that none of this would probably have happened."

"Well in the first place," said Mortie. "They got arrogant. Remember they'd had a lot of success dirtying up people. This little trick they figured was easy. They wanted to muddy the water. Plus, they knew that someone had a little Marijuana business going on and they didn't like it… They were going to move their delivery point anyway and they thought it would keep us occupied. It's very clever, really."

"Mrs. Perlsworth….?"

"Probably…" said Mortie. "A very smart woman… Formidable."

Blackie looked at him. "You still like her, don't you…?"

Mortie sighed. "You're right…. I have to admit it. I have the feeling we'll see her again." He nodded toward the city. Well, the fight goes on. Let's go," he said. They headed back into the city. **End**

54405463R00167

Made in the USA
Columbia, SC
30 March 2019